TED TAYLER

ALL THINGS BRIGHT

TED TAYLER

ALL THINGS
BRIGHT

vinci
books

By Ted Tayler

The Freeman Files

Red Herring Season
Gathering Clouds
Still Standing

Vinci Books

vinci-books.com

Published by Vinci Books Ltd in 2025

1

Chapter One

Monday, 16 July 2018

THE FIRST SIXTY minutes of the working day can often set the tone for the week ahead.

As soon as the team arrived in the office, everyone sensed today was special.

Gus had hardly had time to get comfortable at his desk when the phone rang. It was DI Dai Williams from Cardiff Central.

"Good morning, Dai," said Gus, "I'm praying it's good news?"

"It is, Gus," said Dai. "I don't like Mondays, as a rule, but this feels a decent start to the week for us both. We found Vaughn and Shaun Corbett yesterday evening. They were in Tredegar making a nuisance of themselves knocking on doors just when good folk were on their way to chapel."

"I can update you now on my team's visit to South Wales on Saturday, Dai," said Gus. "After chatting to people in the village who knew Sally Kendall well, we received copies of more recent photographs, which helped us locate Ivan's widow in Crickhowell. But, as you suspected, Sally hadn't strayed far from her roots. She was now Sammy Prosser, a change of name and hair colouring, and handling a responsible job with an estate agent. When questioned, Sammy admitted that their daughter, Alexa, or Lexie, had told her about the two Staffie cross puppies on Sunday afternoon, the day after Ivan disappeared."

"Why on earth didn't she tell us that?" asked Dai Williams. "It would have helped us concentrate our attention further afield from the start."

"Maybe," said Gus, "but Lexie only mentioned it after your officers had left. So, unless you found someone in the village who had seen the Corbett brothers trailing Lexie Kendall and her dogs or conversing with Ivan, you wouldn't have been any closer to linking the matter to Westbury. Certainly not before Monday morning, when police found Ivan's body. I won't deny it would have been vital information in the twenty-four hours that followed, but what's done is done. But, unfortunately, we can't turn back the clock."

"So, mother and daughter moved to Crickhowell?" said Dai. "It's amazing how parochial villages like Pontyclun can be. Mrs Kendall only moved twenty miles away, and yet she may as well have flown to the moon. People from your side of the Bristol Channel have no appreciation of how insular the valleys' old mining communities were. So many houses were tightly packed together, as close as possible to the industry they served. Disease and gossip spread like wildfire, men faced death underground with every passing minute, yet the spirit of the community remained greater in those areas than anywhere else in the world."

"I'm beginning to understand their history," said Gus. "Sally Kendall told my detectives it was her fear of dogs that prompted Ivan to house them in a secure shed on the allotment near the rugby club. That was one secret that came to light after his murder. Lexie revealed another on Saturday afternoon. It caused Ivan to appear quiet and distant in the hours before he left home. The Corbett brothers wanted to buy the puppies. They had offered Ivan five hundred pounds at the rugby club the previous Wednesday when Ivan cleaned its clubhouse windows. He refused their offer. While her father was on his usual Saturday morning task, collecting money from customers, Lexie went to fetch the dogs for their run in the park. They were gone. Lexie found Ivan and got him to call the mobile number on the business card the brothers had left. They were already across the Severn Bridge with the puppies in their van. Lexie was desperate to get them back. The brothers weren't prepared to return them. If Ivan wanted them, he could collect them from Westbury station in return for one thousand pounds in cash."

"Why didn't Ivan report the theft to the police?" asked Dai Williams.

"Because he'd acquired them from a customer who couldn't afford to pay their bill and kept them secret from his wife for a year, I suppose he thought that was out of the question," said Gus. "He hoped to get them back without Sally being any the wiser. But then, Lexie dropped a bombshell as she cried by the phone box after her father heard what it would cost to get the puppies back. She admitted that Martin Jones, who owns the newsagents, had sexually abused her from the age of fourteen to fifteen. In addition, Jones caught her shoplifting, and you can guess the rest."

"I've made a note of the name," said Dai Williams. "You can rest assured that we'll call on Mr Jones before the day's out. What a mess."

"There's more," said Gus. "Lexie moved to Crickhowell with her mother but never settled. She left after her eighteenth birthday and moved to Bridgend. My lads found her in a night-club, where she appears as Satin, an exotic dancer. Your officers believed her to be a 'wild child' who was always in trouble. Martin Jones and several others may have played a part in the persona Lexie portrayed. If your pen is still poised, you might wish to speak to Gethin Hughes. He's the boyfriend who was with Lexie at the station in Pontyclun on Saturday night when Ivan left the village. Whether they had sex before her sixteenth birthday is debatable. In an interview under caution at Cardiff Central, Hughes might provide you with names of other men who knew Lexie before he got involved with her."

"Knew her in the biblical sense, you mean," said Dai Williams. "I've heard that name before. I'm sure Hughes used to play football for a local team. He must be in his mid-thirties now."

"There was a pattern," said Gus, "as my lads discovered when they spoke with Lexie. She ditched her ambitions to be a hairdresser when she left school. Jones, Hughes, and others made her believe that the job she did in Bridgend was all she was good for."

"A sad outcome," said Dai Williams, "does that mean the mother and daughter are no longer in contact with one another?"

"My lads believed that to break the cycle of self-loathing her lifestyle perpetuated, it would benefit Lexie if they reunited her with her mother. The whole sordid story will come out in time. They persuaded Lexie to return with them to Crickhowell."

"We'll do everything in our power to help them through the inevitable trauma that a case such as that attracts," said

Dai. "I can't promise they'll come out unscathed, but it won't be for lack of trying. We didn't do a great job in 2014, but we have an opportunity to put matters right. Thanks, Gus. I'm sure I'll be in touch again soon. We've got enough evidence to proceed with a murder charge. Leave it with us."

"One final question, Dai," said Gus. "Did your officers learn anything further about those dogs?"

"The Corbett brothers had no dogs with them when apprehended," replied Dai Williams. "We'll learn more when we interview them. I don't hold out much hope of Lexie Kendall seeing them again. Ivan Kendall took them to settle a debt, but we would be naïve if we thought it was a selfless gesture. Ivan realised that those dogs would fetch a sizeable sum in several areas close to Pontyclun. The Corbett brothers knew that too, and they might have engaged in the murky world of dog fights. The odds are stacked against those puppies surviving four years and more. I'll update you in due course."

Gus thanked Dai Williams for his help and ended the call. He wondered who he could talk to with inside knowledge of the dogfighting business. It was light years away from the world that Mark Malone frequented in one of their earlier cases. The sad fact was that man's best friend was used to smuggle drugs into the country on that occasion. Now, the nation's favourite pets were getting torn to bits in illegal meets for entertainment. When you thought that criminals couldn't stoop any lower, they proved you wrong time and time again.

Gus picked up the phone. He remembered he'd promised to call Eddie Sinclair in Shaftesbury with any news.

"Eddie?" said Gus, "We finally got your men in the Ivan Kendall case."

"That's great news, Gus," said Eddie, "Was it someone from the traveller's site that I pointed you towards?"

"It was," said Gus. "Vaughn and Shaun Corbett visited an uncle, Jack Ayres, every spring. Ayres came from North Wales, but the family tree had branches everywhere. The brothers spent much of the year in and around Cardiff. That's where they spotted Ivan Kendall's daughter exercising two potentially valuable dogs. At first, they tried to buy them from Ivan, then they grabbed them and brought them to the site near Westbury. To cut a long story short, Ivan travelled to Westbury station to collect the dogs. The brothers demanded one thousand pounds for their safe return. Ivan raised the cash, and when he reached Westbury at midnight that Saturday night, the brothers met him with a different outcome in mind."

"They bludgeoned him to death in the toilet and dropped his body in the fishing lakes," said Eddie Sinclair.

"They kept the dogs and the cash, leaving an amount in Kendall's pockets to confuse you. Why would you think it was a robbery if Kendall still had over sixty quid on him? No wonder you couldn't establish a motive."

"We didn't cover ourselves in glory, that's true," sighed Sinclair. "At least you got them; that's one more case that won't keep me awake at night. Thanks, Gus."

As Eddie spoke, Gus spotted DS Neil Davis giving him the thumbs up. In his other hand, he held the folder relating to the samples he'd collected from the Dilton Marsh traveller's site.

"I might be able to help you sleep even better tonight, Eddie," said Gus. "One of my lads was a motorcycle pursuit rider before he joined the Crime Review Team. He queried how Dyer's accident happened at the point it did. Even in inclement weather, the lorry driver should have been aware of contact with the 125cc motorcycle. The forensic report on samples collected at the roadside after the accident couldn't help identify the vehicle. We knew where the Corbett brothers parked their van during their visits, so another colleague asked forensics to compare samples from the caravan site with material believed to have transferred in the collision to the motorcycle and Dyer's clothing. We've just got confirmation that forensics found a match. Your former colleagues at Westbury can follow up on those findings. It seems clear that the Corbett brother's van forced Sid Dyer off the road that morning. Sid Dyer's local knowledge pointed you towards the fishing lakes far sooner than they had hoped. On their next visit to the area, the brothers took their revenge."

"Another cold-blooded murder solved," said Eddie Sinclair. "D'you know, I'm tempted to call Clive Trainer with the good news, but on second thoughts, I reckon I'll enjoy it alone for a while."

Gus smiled to himself. He wished Eddie Sinclair 'Sweet Dreams' and ended the call. This morning, his team's essential task was to complete the Freeman Files work on the Kendall case. They needed to collate the information Gus wanted to deliver to the ACC.

Blessing Umeh crept across to Gus's desk and sat beside him. She couldn't keep her secret any longer. She leaned closer so the others wouldn't hear.

"You'll think I'm a hopeless case," she whispered. "No matter how I try to excel at things, something always trips me up. Do you remember I mislaid the Freeman Files, and Lydia had to set everything up again? I found a folder with a heading I couldn't remember creating."

"Did it contain that missing file?" asked Gus, "and the NCA goons missed it?"

Blessing nodded.

"I could kiss you," said Gus.

Gus rang Kenneth Truelove at London Road and asked for their meeting to be delayed until eleven o'clock. He needed to secure the contents of that file. Gus couldn't act yet, but he didn't plan to retire with an open cold case against his name, regardless of the obstacles.

LYDIA LOGAN BARRE and Alex Hardy had joined the rest of the team at the start of the new week with plenty to tell them after a weekend in Rotterdam. Somehow, they had to curb their enthusiasm; work came first. While Gus Freeman dealt with DI Williams in Cardiff and DCI Sinclair in Shaftesbury, they updated their copies of the Freeman Files. They ensured that everything relating to the Kendall case was watertight. The files Gus passed to the ACC later that morning must offer the Crown Prosecution Service every chance of a successful outcome.

Lydia and Alex left Chippenham early Friday evening to drive to the port of Harwich. Tucked away on Essex's east coast, Harwich is one of the county's most historic towns. The 'Mayflower' set sail from there in 1620 across the Atlantic to the New World.

They were tired after a journey that took four hours with the high volume of summer traffic on the motorways. Ahead of them lay another seven hours aboard the car ferry that delivered them to the Hook of Holland. Alex was asleep within minutes of the ferry leaving port. Lydia dozed for a while, but it was difficult not to think about why she was there.

It had taken several years to find her birth mother, Eleanor Scott, and they now enjoyed a warm, friendly relationship. Neither demanded too much from the other. Lydia would always consider Mr and Mrs Logan as Mum and Dad. They had adopted her within weeks of Lydia's birth. Nothing could weaken that bond. Lydia accepted Eleanor's reasons for giving her up for adoption, and they were moving forward.

On the occasions they met after initial contact through a mediator, Eleanor gradually told Lydia more details about her father. Chidozie Barre. He was twenty-one, a sailor from Yaba, near Lagos, Nigeria. He'd wandered into the gift shop in George Street, Edinburgh, searching for a souvenir for his mother.

Eleanor and Chidozie had two days together before he sailed from the port of Leith. The handsome young man who stole Eleanor's heart had no idea that their brief liaison produced a bonny baby daughter that Eleanor called Lisa Marie nine months later.

As soon as she learned her birth father's name, Lydia wanted to discover where he'd gone after leaving Edinburgh. With Alex's help, they'd traced him to Rotterdam. When the ferry landed in the Hook of Holland, the A20 highway would take them into the city within half an hour.

Alex had booked them into a floating hotel on Bierstraat, only a five-minute walk via Wijnhaven from the 'Lady Eleanor' where her father lived and worked. Chidozie Barre opened a bar in April 2016, just around the corner from the Maritime Museum in Leuvehaven.

Lydia knew that sometime on Saturday, she would meet her biological father for the first time. Alex had warned her not to expect too much. They hadn't given Chidozie any indication they were coming to Rotterdam. He didn't know he had a daughter of twenty-five. He might not want to know.

Lydia listened to Alex's words, but she had made up her mind. She was curious to see the face of the man whose DNA determined the way she looked. What similarities were there in their physical make-up? Eleanor said he was tall. That was something they had in common. Chidozie had a smile that lit up the room, too. What kind of person was he now, after the trauma he'd suffered in the shipwreck? Was he quiet, loud, moody, or full of life?

Lydia wanted to ask why he never came back to Edinburgh. Was it a deliberate act to stay away or just chance? She needed to understand and allow him to explain himself. It was important to hear his side of the story. Everything she thought she knew came from Eleanor. If he'd realised he'd fathered a child, how would he have reacted? Would he have been like Eleanor and thought he wasn't ready for the responsibility then?

Lydia had never held a grudge against either of her birth parents. After meeting Eleanor and realising that it was enough to be friends, she redoubled her efforts to find her father. Lydia wanted to show Chidozie that there was nothing to forgive. After such an extended period, they couldn't have a genuine father-daughter relationship. Still, she hoped there would be the possibility of developing a similar understanding that now existed between her and Eleanor.

Most of all, this weekend was for closure. Lydia didn't want to look back in years to come and regretted not taking this final step. Sleep claimed her at last, and they were only minutes from the port when Alex woke her.

"Excited?" he asked.

"Nervous," she'd replied.

"You needn't worry whether you inherited your father's sea legs," said Alex.

"I had a lot on my mind," said Lydia, "before I dropped off to sleep. I know one thing, I'm starving. It's ages since we had a bite to eat."

Alex drove the car on the last leg of the journey. He'd ridden his motorcycle on holidays abroad, so Lydia was happy to let him cope with the traffic and drive on the right.

"I thought the M25 was bad," she groaned," this is a nightmare."

"We can turn off the main drag and find a place to eat," said Alex. "It's always this busy, but you'll be in a better mood once you've had your first cup of coffee and bacon and apple pancakes."

Alex was right, as usual. However, they both felt more human when they arrived in Bierstraat and parked near the hotel.

"What time do you think our room will be ready?" asked Lydia.

"Why, what did you have in mind?" asked Alex.

Lydia thumped his arm.

"I was wondering whether we could drop off our bags and take a walk to the Maritime Museum. However, before venturing inside, I want to check out the area and walk past the bar. What time does the 'Lady Eleanor' open?"

"Ten o'clock," said Alex, "according to the information I found online. The bar closes at one in the morning."

"That's a long day," said Lydia. "Chi-Chi couldn't possibly cover the whole day. I wonder which half of the day he works?"

"If we're right in our assumption that he chose the bar's location because of its proximity to the Museum, then he'll be there in an hour. You will see him raising the shutters."

"What do you think we should do first?" asked Lydia.

"You wait in the car. I'll go across to the hotel and check on the room."

Lydia sat and waited.

She had done her homework, too, just like her father. Rotterdam has evolved from a down-at-heel port city into one of Europe's favourite getaways.

Lydia smiled as she saw Alex trotting back to the car. She'd seen his face when he looked at the bill in the café earlier. Some things were far more expensive here than back in the UK. Yet, the online reviews she had read thought Rotterdam offered value for money. It certainly had plenty of museums and galleries to visit, only a ten-minute walk from where she sat if the weather was poor. They didn't have to worry on that score today.

"Three o'clock," said Alex, "but they have agreed to store our bags for us. Let's take advantage of that and then return to get checked in this afternoon."

Ten minutes later, they were on their way.

Chapter Two

"THERE," cried Lydia, grabbing Alex by the arm. "Can you see anyone inside?"

Alex knew the feeling would return in his arm in time.

They had turned the corner to enter the street where Chidozie had his bar. The 'Lady Eleanor' was on a narrow side street off Wijnhaven. Parked bicycles littered the pavement on either side of the bar. A loading bay for two vehicles was empty in front of the modern, bright-looking bar.

Alex and Lydia strolled along the pavement on the opposite side of the street. Three four-seater stained wooden benches sat outside the large plate-glass window. The interior blazed with light. The colour scheme of red, white, and black was nothing like Lydia's image in her head since she learned that Chidozie was living and working here.

"It looks so smart and clean," said Lydia.

"What did you expect," said Alex, "ye olde Smuggler's Tavern? Look around us. The entire district has that sleek, industrial-chic look. It's only the bikes that make the place untidy."

"I can't see him inside," said Lydia. "Not that I know what he looks like. Perhaps he's upstairs in the flat, looking at us."

Lydia stood back from the pavement's edge and peered up at the windows on the upper floors. She saw nothing.

"It's still early," said Alex. "Let's tour the Museum Park and the other attractions. Then, we can come back around lunchtime."

"I downloaded a suggested route onto my phone before we left Chippenham," said Lydia. "We can reach Central Station in ten minutes. It's one of the coolest stations in Europe, and it's supposed to set the artistic mood for our day. I'll admire the beautiful architecture while you grab us a coffee."

"You've got it worked out, haven't you," said Alex.

"If only," said Lydia. "I'm so nervous now. I can't remember what I wanted to ask or say to him. What if he doesn't even speak to me? What if we picked the only weekend in the year when he's flown away on holiday?"

"We'll follow the route on your phone and take your mind off your Dad by seeing the sights this city offers."

The station was everything Lydia hoped it would be, and the coffee was delicious.

"The next place on this quick tour is one I'm dying to see," she said as they left the station.

Alex walked beside her, and as they turned the corner, he had to admit it impressed him.

"Wow! A yellow pedestrian bridge connecting the two sides of the city,"

After exploring the Luchtsingel pedestrian bridge, they returned to the roundabout and walked south.

"This is a busy district," said Alex, taking in the sights. "With cafes, restaurants, and shopping malls on both sides of the street. I love the canal here."

"If we follow these canals, we'll soon return to Leuvehaven and our hotel. The Maritime Museum is just over there. We ought to visit it. I wondered whether it played a part in the bar's location."

One look at the variety of exhibits on offer on the notice boards outside the Museum meant that they wouldn't do it justice unless they spent several hours inside.

"Perhaps we should add it to our list of things to do tomorrow?" asked Lydia. "We might have a free day if things don't go to plan."

"Don't give up just yet," said Alex. "Who's that man explaining something to a group of visitors waiting outside?"

Lydia spun around. Through the crowds, she spotted a tall, handsome man. Lydia tried to remain calm as she studied the man's face, hair, and eyes. The way he stood looked familiar, and he had flecks of grey at his temples. The man could be in his late forties or early fifties. His eyes shone as he spoke to the visitors. The subject was clearly something he enjoyed. One child in the group asked a question or passed a comment. The man threw back his head and laughed. The smile that followed was just how Eleanor described it.

Lydia studied the man's clothes. She was convinced this was Chidozie Barre. The years he'd spent at sea had kept him fit. Chidozie was still lean and muscular. His quarterzip navy blue sailor's sweater and navy slacks oozed class. Lydia smiled. Forget Idris Elba as James Bond. Chidozie Barre would slip into the role like a hand into a glove.

As she daydreamed of her father starring on the big

screen, he looked over the heads of the visitor group and stared straight at her.

"There's nothing for it, Lydia," said Alex. "You have to walk across and talk to him. He looks as if he's seen a ghost."

Lydia made her way through the queuing tourists, followed by Alex.

"Je gezicht komt bekend voor," said the man.

"I'm afraid I don't speak Dutch," said Lydia.

"Your face looks familiar. I recognise your accent too. You are from Scotland."

"I am. My mother was born in Edinburgh, and so was I."

Alex stepped forward and steadied a shaky Chidozie Barre as realisation dawned.

"We should find a café," said Alex. "You need to sit. You've had a shock."

Chidozie pointed behind Alex but didn't speak. He continued to stare at the beautiful coffee-coloured face of the girl with the shock of red hair. Her voice had just transported him back twenty-six years to a time he would never forget.

When Chidozie and Lydia had sat down, Alex went inside the café to order drinks.

"Is that your husband?"

"Not yet," said Lydia, "we're work colleagues back in England."

"I don't understand how you came to be here today. What are you called?"

"The family that adopted me named me Lydia,"

"The beautiful one," said Chidozie. "They chose well."

"I've searched for you for several years," said Lydia. "As

soon as we learned that you opened a bar and called it the 'Lady Eleanor', I knew I should come to meet you."

"Why didn't I know of you? Why did Eleanor not look for me?"

Lydia explained the eighteen-year-old Eleanor Scott faced problems because of her family's reaction after learning that she was pregnant. They refused to take in a baby fathered by a black man. Eleanor didn't know the ship's name and couldn't support a baby alone. So she gave her baby up for adoption.

"We left the port of Leith twenty-four hours after the last time I saw Eleanor," said Chidozie. "I was at sea for five months before I took the presents I'd bought in her shop to my mother back home in Yaba. I thought of Eleanor every day and told my mother that I'd met a beautiful Scottish girl. She said that the memory of my first love would always stay with me. Of course, because I had chosen a life at sea, there would be other girls in other ports, but in Yaba, there were girls from families that my parents knew who would be more suitable for marriage."

"Did you marry a local girl?" asked Lydia.

Chidozie shook his head.

"I never married. I was the youngest in the family, and my three older sisters married and gave my parents a dozen grandchildren between them. Although my father wished for a son to carry on the family name, he never pressured me into an arranged marriage. Both my parents are dead now. I haven't returned to Nigeria since I attended their burials."

"Why didn't you return to Scotland to find Eleanor if she was the only one for you?" asked Lydia.

"I've asked myself that question many times," sighed Chidozie. "We never spoke of love in the two days we spent together. After we made love in the park that night, there was no understanding that it was a commitment to a lasting relationship. It was just a moment we shared. It felt inevitable we'd never meet again. How could we? My ship would unlikely return to Edinburgh for a year, maybe more. As it was, circumstances with the shipping company I worked for meant that we only landed at a British port on two more occasions, years after we first met. America, Asia, and Africa were places I visited far more than in Europe. As the years passed, I accepted that a girl as pretty as Eleanor would have found someone else. What a fool I would look if I flew to Scotland and visited the gift shop with a bunch of red roses to learn that she had left ages ago to get married. How on earth did you ever find me, Lydia?"

Lydia explained how she had traced her birth mother and that she and Eleanor were friends.

"I spent so many years with the Logans that they will always be my Mum and Dad. As I got to know Eleanor, my birth mother, I asked her to tell me about my father. She told me you were a merchant sailor from Nigeria and that your friends called you Chi-Chi. We traced the details of the reefer you worked on through maritime records in London. Alex and I then followed your career at sea right through to the time of the shipwreck."

"The typhoon was too powerful," said Chidozie. "I'd never experienced such winds. We didn't stand a chance. The Coast Guard was so far away that I had given up any hopes of rescue. The authorities in Manila believed that everyone perished. I prayed that night as I'd never prayed before. Then a freighter battled its way through treacherous seas to reach us. They had seen the final distress signal that I sent, and although they were searching for a needle in a haystack, they arrived just as we were preparing to face death. They plucked twelve of us from the waves as we clung to the two life rafts we had roped together."

"We learned from your former shipping company that after that dreadful ordeal, you never went to sea again," said Alex.

"The freighter that rescued us carried us into the port of Da Nang," said Chidozie. "I went with my colleagues to the hospital to see if they were getting the care they needed. Then, exhausted but uninjured, I flew as far away from the South China Sea as possible to spend a month in Dubai, recuperating. Then, I thought I'd try my luck in America."

"That's when we picked up the trail again," said Lydia, "after a lifetime at sea and reaching the senior position of First Mate, you suddenly became an expert cocktail maker. Where did that talent come from?"

Chidozie threw his head back and laughed again.

"I needed the money to live," said Chidozie, "I don't drink alcohol, but mixing drinks to a recipe isn't rocket science. I learned fast, and because I stayed sober, I avoided the muggers and racists I bumped into when I walked home to my apartment. The move to Hamburg came at the right time. The same problems existed, but life was more relaxed than in New York. When you're a single man, if you don't drink or gamble, it's possible to save to afford your own business. So I kept my eye on properties in Hamburg and here in Rotterdam. When the right place became available, I made an offer and moved here, changing the bar's name from 'The Hideaway' to 'Lady Eleanor'. It was the right choice because it helped you find me. I have a daughter now. It feels strange, but I love it."

"We walked by the bar earlier this morning," said Alex. "I knew it was you as soon as I spotted you outside the Museum. Do you work there?"

"I volunteer my time," said Chidozie. "It's the least I can do. The sea is still important to me, despite how my career ended. I'm here whenever they need me from eleven o'clock until three. I work in my bar in the evenings. How long are you staying in Rotterdam?"

"Our ferry leaves the Hook tomorrow evening," said Lydia.

"Where are you staying tonight?"

"At one of the floating hotels a few minutes' walk from here," said Alex. "Check-in is at three. We're going to have lunch and then spend an hour resting at the hotel. Neither of us slept much on the ferry last night."

"Will you come to the 'Lady Eleanor' this evening?" asked Chidozie.

"Of course," said Lydia.

"I'll get a staff member to cover for me later. I will take you to dinner tonight. On this trip, there won't be another opportunity."

"That would be great," said Lydia.

"I have questions to ask, Lydia," said Chidozie. "but I should get back to the Maritime Museum. This is strange and new to me. What do we do now? Shake hands or hug?"

Lydia hugged Chidozie. The two men shook hands.

"What is your name?" asked Chidozie.

"Alex Hardy, sir," said Alex. "Detective Sergeant Alex Hardy. Pleased to meet you at last."

"Until tonight, then, Lydia," said Chidozie Barre.

"I was Lydia Logan until I met Eleanor and learned my birth father's name," said Lydia. "When I travelled south from Scotland to work with the same team as Alex, I made it official. I'm Lydia Logan Barre now."

"That's wonderful," smiled Chidozie, "even your name is beautiful."

With a wave, her father eased his way through the customers waiting to enter the Museum and started back to work. Lydia and Alex set off on a ten-minute walk that would bring them to the Market Hall.

"The building is enormous," said Alex, "and another must-see place in Rotterdam. We'll find food stalls, restaurants, and shops galore. There's bound to be somewhere that we can get lunch. In the Square in front of the Market Hall are the yellow Cube Houses, an icon of Rotterdam architecture."

"I was thinking of those yellow houses earlier while you were in the hotel," said Lydia. "They're on my list of things to visit. Perhaps we can look inside one after we've eaten?"

"Breakfast seems a long time ago," said Alex, "and all this walking is telling on my leg.

"We've got until three o'clock, Alex," said Lydia, linking her arm through his. "Lean on me, and we'll cross the Erasmus Bridge and admire the Mass River and the Rotterdam skyline as we eat our meal."

Ninety minutes later, the couple was ready to tackle the next stage of their tour of the best attractions. Lydia wanted to see as much of her father's home town as possible this weekend, but she didn't want Alex to get overtired.

"Let's save our legs for a while," she said. "we can take a water taxi to get us around in comfort. That will be the best way to fill the final ninety minutes before check-in at the hotel."

They returned to the floating hotel and stowed their gear in their room.

"What now?" asked Alex.

"I'm shattered," said Lydia. "Set the alarm on your phone for six-thirty. The last one asleep is a sissy."

Alex was first to wake up and slipped out of bed and into the shower. Lydia joined him minutes later.

"Chidozie told us he never married," said Lydia. "That's so sad. I hope he isn't lonely."

"When we saw how he was with the line of Museum visitors, I think he's the gregarious type, don't you? I'm sure his bar will be livelier when he's in there, and who knows, he might have met someone special here in Rotterdam."

"Maybe his late mother was right," said Lydia. "He had a girl in every port. Perhaps he's left a long line of broken-hearted females in cities worldwide."

"I don't think you should ask him that this evening," said Alex. "You don't want to push too hard."

"Okay," said Lydia. "I prepared a long list of questions before we left home, and this morning most of them flew away on the breeze. I dreamt of Chidozie telling me that Eleanor was his first love and he never forgot her. That romantic idea was in my head before we learned about the bar's name. While listening to Eleanor telling me how they met, I imagined them finding one another again after so many years and everything being sweetness and light. It was unrealistic, but they were the exact words he used this morning. He even said that naming the bar 'Lady Eleanor' had helped me find him."

"You must remember how Eleanor spoke about him," said Alex. "She made a life without Chidozie Barre and was happy with her lot. The two of you have moved forward as friends, which works for you. When we get home, talk to your mother, better still visit her, and speak about this week-end. Eleanor might decide to come here to renew their acquaintance, or she might get in touch by phone or letter. After so many years, Eleanor might be happy to learn Chi-Chi's alive and well but not want contact with him."

"You're right. It's Eleanor's choice," said Lydia. "I need to rein in my enthusiasm. I'm letting my imagination run wild."

"The most important thing tonight, and for what free time we have left tomorrow, is for you and your father to agree on what relationship you can have in the future. Once that's sorted, you can worry over what Eleanor and Chidozie want to happen."

"I'm so lucky," said Lydia. "I have a father in Aberdeen, another in Rotterdam, and if they can't offer me enough wise counsel, then I can rely on you to keep me on the right path. I love you, Alex."

"I love you too, Lydia. Now, this shower is running cold. I vote we dry ourselves and get dressed. We must try to look as elegant as your father if we're dining with him tonight. I know you brought enough clothes for a week, but I'm a smart-casual guy when I'm not at work. I leave my suits in the wardrobe when I go on holiday. You must decide which shirt looks the smartest from my limited selection."

The view that greeted them differed from this morning when they stood across the road from Chi-Chi's bar at seven-thirty. Someone sat on every seat on the benches outside, and couples and small groups congregated on the pavement. Conversation and laughter filled the air. Through the crowd, Lydia could see the bar was busy inside too. The various male and female staff members scurried from table to table, taking orders or delivering food and drink to eager customers.

Chidozie favoured a simple uniform of crisp white shirts and black slacks, regardless of gender. Lydia searched for Chidozie, but she couldn't see him at first.

"Fancy a beer?" asked Alex. "Let's get a cold one and stand outside on the pavement. It will be too warm indoors.

We'll tell the bar staff we've arrived. Chi-Chi could be upstairs getting ready or dealing with customers at the back of the room. We can't see every dark corner from here."

Alex and Lydia crossed the road and went inside the 'Lady Eleanor' for the first time. Lydia looked for a senior member of staff. Most staff working this evening were teenagers, but a middle-aged, blonde-haired woman was hovering by the bar, keeping her eye on everything. Lydia heard her issuing orders to her charges as they rushed past. Her accent was Dutch.

"Excuse me," said Lydia, "we're meeting Chidozie here. Has he arrived yet?"

"You must be Lydia," said the woman, "I'm Rosa. He's still upstairs in the apartment. He won't be five minutes."

Alex arrived with two cold lagers.

"We'll be outside," said Lydia. "It's too nice an evening to stay indoors."

Rosa smiled and resumed her vigil.

While Rosa was on deck, Alex reckoned the 'Lady Eleanor' was a well-oiled machine that maximised Chidozie Barre's profits.

"Your father chose an ideal location," said Alex when they were back outside. "With these narrow streets, most traffic will be on foot or two wheels. The four-wheel commercial transport will be early morning waste collection and morning deliveries to the restaurants and bars. The bar's sheltered from the wind too."

"Did you catch what Rosa said?" asked Lydia. "He's still upstairs in *the* apartment."

"You're jumping to conclusions again," said Alex.

"Do I look alright?" asked Lydia. "I'm nervous. What if Chidozie thinks my skirt is too short?"

"It looks fine from where I'm standing," said Alex.

"You've got great legs, Lydia. Even Gus Freeman couldn't object to what you're wearing tonight. It might be too much for the Crime Review Team office, but it's perfect for an evening in town."

Lydia tugged at her black leather skirt and tried to convince herself that it was decent. Her loose-fitting bright-orange, brown and yellow top drew most men's attention away from her skirt in any case. Not for the first time, she was the only girl in the vicinity with corkscrew curls of ginger hair.

Alex felt happy with Lydia's choice of a pale blue shirt with a button-down collar. He was thankful she hadn't opted for his white shirt. He would never have escaped the 'Lady Eleanor', although the tips from waiting on tables would have helped pay the eye-watering prices for two bottles of lager.

There was a sudden hush on the pavement behind them. Something had caused the conversation level to drop. Lydia turned to look over her shoulder. It was her secret agent emerging from the bar's interior. Chidozie left any Western suits he possessed in the wardrobe. His navy blue outfit was stylish and based on a traditional agbada. The top was wide-sleeved with elaborate gold embroidery that covered the shoulders. The undervest was a loose, round-neck, sleeveless smock, and his trousers were close-fitting, ankle-length, and narrow-bottomed.

"He knows how to make an entrance," said Alex.

"I don't think his regular customers have seen him in anything resembling his national dress before," said Lydia.

Chidozie Barre kissed Lydia on both cheeks and shook Alex by the hand.

He stood back to admire his daughter's outfit.

"I can see now why I needed to adjust my kiss to land on your cheek," he grinned.

"Four-inch heels, Chidozie," said Alex, "I need a step."

"My apologies for keeping you waiting," said Chidozie. "Rosa will look after things here while we go to a favourite restaurant of mine. Our Uber Netherlands vehicle will be here in one minute."

"Rosa seems very efficient," said Alex.

"She worked for 'The Hideaway' when I bought the place. The previous owner advised me I wouldn't find a more honest, hard-working employee in the city. So, I took her on. I wouldn't be without her."

The taxi arrived, and Chidozie didn't expand on the comment. After a delicious meal, they returned to find the 'Lady Eleanor' packed with customers.

"Is it always this busy?" asked Lydia.

"We offer value for money," said Chidozie, "a wider selection of beers than most places in the area, plus our chef prepares the best fresh fish dishes in Rotterdam. In high summer, the number of tourists swells the customers. Trade will drop off in the autumn when we take our annual holiday. Everyone needs to refresh themselves before the Christmas and New Year mayhem."

"Where do you spend your holidays?" asked Lydia.

"Dubai," said Chidozie. "It was my refuge after the shipwreck, and I return there every autumn to give thanks."

"I'm sorry if I asked a lot of questions of you this evening," said Lydia.

"It's only natural," her father replied. "Where's Rosa? I want to tell her we'll be upstairs in the apartment. There's nowhere for us to have a quiet conversation here tonight. People will drift away in an hour, but we get a regular influx of late-night drinkers that finish work at nearby businesses and then drop in for a drink and a chat."

Alex and Lydia waited by a door marked 'Privaat', which was self-explanatory. Chidozie talked to customers at tables as he made his way towards the back of the bar.

"He's popular, isn't he?" said Alex. "Half the people in the restaurant knew him too, not just the management."

"I learned superficial things this evening," said Lydia, "and he steered the conversation in such a way that it was two-way traffic. I thought with the experience I've gained working with experts such as Gus and the rest of you. He'd be putty in my hands."

"Now there's something we've discovered without asking questions," said Alex, nodding to the other side of the bar.

Rosa and Chidozie were deep in conversation. Her hand rested casually on his upper arm, and the look between them suggested their relationship was a million miles from employer and employee.

Chidozie leaned forward to kiss Rosa on the lips and then started back across the room.

"I've promised Rosa we will return when the rush is over," he said, "I will introduce you properly then."

When they reached Chidozie's apartment, Lydia could tell from the living room and kitchenette that this wasn't a bachelor pad. The furnishings and the overall ambience confirmed what they'd seen downstairs. Chidozie and Rosa were a couple.

"I have never been a hermit," said Chidozie. Nevertheless, he spotted how Lydia analysed the set-up within seconds of entering the room.

"I hope that doesn't shock you, Lydia. Rosa isn't the first woman I lived with over the years. It's true that I never married and that I have never forgotten Eleanor. I wasn't trying to deceive you."

"You don't need to apologise," said Lydia. "We're still strangers. If we continue meeting and talking, we will learn more about each other. My first few conversations with Eleanor were the same. Nothing we disclosed ever displeased or upset us enough to stop meeting. We came out the other side as friends. You and I have taken the first tentative steps on the same journey. So far, nothing makes me wish I hadn't come here this weekend."

"I'm glad you did," said Chidozie. "It was a shock for me and Rosa too. She understood that I had lovers in my past; she was no innocent when married as a young woman. After her divorce, she moved from Amsterdam to work at 'The Hideaway', and she was alone when I arrived. We hit it off within a month of me opening the 'Lady Eleanor', and we've lived together ever since. Rosa will need time to adjust to the fact that I have a daughter too. Now, let me get you a drink. What will it be?"

"We heard that a jenever was popular," said Lydia.

Chidozie laughed.

"We serve it straight from the freezer downstairs. Some prefer it straight from the bottle, like drinking vodka, but most customers mix it with vermouth and other ingredients to make it less lethal."

"Perhaps we should have a coffee instead," said Alex. "You don't drink alcohol, Chidozie, and Lydia and I already had several glasses of wine with our meal."

"I understand," said Chidozie, "you've had a long day. No doubt you want to return to your hotel before this place closes."

"I'm only twenty-five," said Lydia, "and although Alex is ten years older, we can still keep pace. We intend to be here when the shutters close. I've waited a long time for this weekend."

"Rosa enjoys a quality brandy," said Chidozie, checking the drinks cabinet, "so, two Coffee Royale's it shall be, and an Americano for me."

Chidozie prepared the drinks, and Lydia and Alex relaxed on the large sofa as Chidozie told them how he had learned his trade in the cocktails bar in New York. He had an unlimited supply of funny stories. Lydia wasn't sure after the second drink, whether it was the memories that made her giggle or the generous measures of brandy that Chidozie added.

"It's after midnight," said Alex. "We should get downstairs, or Rosa will think you've abandoned her."

"There should be more room now," said Chidozie, "the mad rush is at an end."

When they got downstairs, Rosa was behind the bar. The waiting staff had gone home, and the chef sat at the end of the bar reading a newspaper. His empty glass suggested he would soon be on his way.

No customers sat outside, despite the warm night, but the bar still contained a healthy number of people enjoying a late-night drink. Alex and Lydia sat on stools by the bar as Chidozie joined Rosa.

"Did you both enjoy your meal?" asked Rosa.

"It was excellent," said Alex. "I'm sure you know the restaurant well?"

"It's our favourite here in Rotterdam," said Rosa, looking at Chidozie. "Although, he would say the restaurant in Dubai is a touch better."

"When you eat at a five-star restaurant, it's not worth comparing," laughed Chidozie. "They each have their minor differences, but why split hairs trying to choose which one is better than the other?"

The chef folded his newspaper and eased himself off his stool.

"I'm away to my bed, boss," he said. "I'll see you tomorrow."

"Good night, Lucas," said Chidozie. "You put in a good shift today: thank you, my friend. I got great feedback from the tables as I walked through this evening. The seafood platter was a firm favourite."

Lucas nodded and left the bar.

"Perhaps we can taste how good his food is tomorrow," said Lydia.

"We're lucky to have him," said Rosa. "I don't think we'll be able to match the salary a bigger outfit could offer Lucas."

"Let's not discuss our chef, Rosa," said Chidozie, "Lucas Romeijn will leave us when he's ready. I'll not stand in his way. Let me make the introductions. Rosa de Vries, I am pleased to introduce Lydia Logan Barre, my daughter. Her gentleman friend is Alex Hardy. They are with the English police, but we have nothing to fear."

"You idiot," said Rosa. "What will they think of us? Welcome, Lydia. It stunned me when Chidozie came home from the Museum to tell me the news—stunned but happy for him. I hope you will continue to visit us. You are both welcome in our home, any time."

"I didn't think this weekend could get any better," said Lydia, leaning over the bar to hug Rosa. "Thank you. It means the world to me."

"What will you do tomorrow?" asked Rosa.

"We planned to continue sightseeing before lunch," said Alex.

"Then we're coming here to eat," said Lydia. "If it's okay with you, we'll spend our last few hours in Rotterdam with you both until it's time to drive to the Hook to catch the car ferry."

"That's settled then," said Chidozie. "Only one thing to do before you finally take your leave. You must tell us when you'll be back."

"We'll exchange contact details tomorrow," said Lydia. "We've used up several days holiday trying to find you, but we'll be able to take time off before Christmas."

"When we've closed this place for a fortnight, why not fly to Dubai, and I'll collect you from the airport," said Chidozie. "You can stay with us. We'll visit that restaurant Rosa was keen to tell you about."

"It sounds exciting," said Lydia. "Of course, we'd love to come if possible."

"You will make it happen," said Chidozie, "I know I can rely on you."

"Where do you stay when you're out there?" asked Alex.

"Chidozie bought an apartment by the Marina when he was there in 2007," said Rosa. "It was a wonderful investment."

"I recuperated in a small place nearby after the ship-wreck and decided I'd had enough danger at sea for two lifetimes. So, I contacted the shipping company and collected my outstanding wages, holiday pay, and long-service gratuity. Finally, I could buy an apartment in a new build that would set me back half a million euros today."

"Wow," said Lydia, "that's amazing."

An hour later, Alex and Lydia unsteadily returned to the hotel. Chidozie was right. It had been a long day. They both slept well.

They just about made the check-out time of eleven

o'clock from the floating hotel. It cut short the sightseeing tour, and Alex elected for water taxi trips to avoid adding to the ache he felt in his leg from the exercise yesterday.

Sunday afternoon was a pleasant, relaxed affair, just like Sunday afternoons with friends should be. But, after the lunch Lucas prepared for them, Lydia hoped that her father could somehow hang on to the talented chef for a bit longer.

It was difficult saying goodbyes to Chidozie and Rosa and leaving the 'Lady Eleanor' to return to the port to catch the ferry. However, it had to be done if they wished to return to Harwich in time to arrive at the Crime Review Team office at nine. Alex planned to catch up on sleep on Monday night if Lydia kept him awake on the ferry because she was too excited to sleep. So when they arrived back in Chippenham early this morning, there was only one matter to get sorted.

Lydia knew that she had to tell Eleanor that they had met Chidozie.

Should they mention the name of the bar? What if Eleanor searched online and found it for herself? How would she react?

Alex had noticed Chidozie's slight frown when they had exchanged contact details. Had he hoped Lydia would give him those for Eleanor Scott too? Rosa and Chidozie were an item, that's for sure. Alex had to watch that Lydia's romantic notions didn't drive a wedge between the couple. Eleanor and Chidozie had moved on with their lives over the past quarter of a century. There was no turning back the clock.

Chapter Three

GUS GLANCED at the clock on the office wall. It was almost ten-thirty.

"Do we have everything ready to take to London Road," he asked.

"Five minutes, guv," said Lydia. "Sorry, I'm still buzzing after the weekend."

"I look forward to hearing about it later in the week," said Gus. "If time allows. Until I've met with the ACC, I have no clue which case is in his in-tray for us this time."

Five minutes later, the relevant files were ready. Gus walked to the lift and headed to the car park. As soon as he was safely off the premises, Lydia gave the gang a minute-by-minute account of their adventure. It was too good to keep quiet any longer.

Meanwhile, Gus eased the Focus into the mid-morning traffic and headed for Devizes.

The sun always shines on the righteous, he thought, as he pulled off the London Road and into the visitor's car park. The upstairs window at the far left of the building caught the full blast of the morning sun. In his customary position, Kenneth Truelove stood, jacketless, staring at the worker ants.

Gus always found it difficult to gauge whether the ACC was in a good mood from his vantage point on the car park asphalt. Discretion persuaded Gus to trot up the steps and get upstairs as soon as possible. He would keep the delay at Seend because of roadworks to himself.

It was so regular an excuse that he didn't think the ACC believed a word even though genuine. As he reached the admin area on the first floor, the clock had ticked to seven minutes past eleven. Gus gave a brief wave to Vera and Kassie, pointed to his watch, and tapped on the ACC's door.

"Come," said Kenneth Truelove.

"Geoff Mercer not here this morning, sir?" asked Gus realising he was the ACC's only visitor.

"Mercer has been and gone, Freeman," said the ACC. "He appreciates how busy my role is these days."

Ouch, thought Gus. No need to guess which mood he's in.

"My team struggled to get the details together in time," said Gus. "Neil Davis and Luke Sherman worked on the case in South Wales on Saturday. We should congratulate them for going the extra mile to tie up loose ends on the case, plus they reunited Mrs Kendall and her daughter. An excellent result, I'm sure you'll agree."

"Well, if you put it like that, I suppose," said the ACC. He was out of his seat and back by the window.

"Do you believe Cardiff Central can pin the murder on these Corbett characters?"

"They have more than enough, sir," said Gus. "West-bury is also in receipt of fresh evidence showing that the

Corbett brothers knocked Sid Dyer off his motorcycle with their van too. Everyone's a winner."

"Not me," said Kenneth Truelove, "It's me who has to explain the unauthorised overtime you sanctioned on Saturday. The bean counters don't credit us for solving a murder on the books for four years. They're more interested in the financial implications. As for Dyer, that got ruled an accident. Now you've uncovered evidence that proves it was deliberate, is that right?"

Gus nodded.

"There you are," groaned the ACC. "That will rebound on me too. Unravelling the packaged paperwork on that caper will cost a pretty penny. Also, it doesn't show the original verdict from the coroner in a good light. I wish you looked before you leap, Freeman. We spent years fostering good relations with various branches of the justice department, and in a matter of months, you ride roughshod through the lot of them, highlighting their inefficiencies."

"We do our best, sir," said Gus. "Might I ask a question?"

"Does it involve an expense that will bankrupt the force?"

"I hope not, sir. I was thinking about the dogs when I was telling DI Williams the good news this morning."

Kenneth Truelove had returned to his desk and was leafing through the files in the folder on his desk.

"Bubble and Squeak?"

"The very same, sir," said Gus. "Dai Williams is interviewing the brothers as we speak. He anticipates requiring several sessions to bring them to their senses. The chances are that the dogs didn't last long after Ivan Kendall's murder. There was no sign of any dogs when the brothers got picked up in Tredegar."

"Why the concern?" asked the ACC.

"After investigating the Malone case, I realised that dogs were important to people in more ways than I imagined. My parents never had pets in the home when I was a kid. I didn't think to ask whether it was because we couldn't afford them or they had an aversion to animals. Then I uncovered that dreadful drug smuggling business where innocent pups had quantities of heroin sewn inside their bodies. When we dug into this latest case, another opportunity for the dogs' illegal use proved to be the motive for Kendall's death. I had no idea dogfighting was still an issue, especially since the Dangerous Dogs Act passed in 1991."

"What do you think you can do, Freeman," said Kenneth Truelove. "It's not the Crime Review Team's role to chase organisers of illegal dog fights. Geoff Mercer has people he can assign to that dirty business when it raises its head on our patch."

"Where is Geoff Mercer, anyway?" asked Gus. "It is ages since I had a conversation with him. We keep missing one another here at London Road."

The ACC was wandering again. He stood by the window and rested on the sill.

"There was a genuine reason for his absence at first," said the ACC. "Geoff attended a course on a new initiative that the Police and Crime Commissioner championed. The usual rubbish. Typical of Mercer, he shone in the sessions he attended and attracted someone's attention. West Mercia is headhunting him for a vacant Assistant Chief Constable position."

"That's good news, isn't it?" said Gus. "Although I'll be sorry to see him go."

"It was selfish of me, I admit," sighed Kenneth Truelove, "but, as you know, I'd set my heart on retirement at the end of next year. After Sandra Plunkett's demise, the PCC twisted my arm to become Acting Chief Constable until the dust settled and the right candidate turned up."

"You were hoping to keep Geoff Mercer at London Road by putting his name forward to the PCC, am I right?"

"Yes, my wife reluctantly agreed to put up with a Chief Constable working after he'd agreed to retire and start cruising the high seas. I informed the PCC that I would continue if he needed me, provided he made the promotion permanent. I was biding my time to engineer Mercer's upgrade when the PCC suddenly dropped the diversity initiative on me. When I looked around at my senior team, the only name that made sense was Mercer. So, I told the PCC Geoff would be the right chap to attend. Of course, the glowing comments that have filtered back from the course mean that the PCC now says my choice was inspired and keeps telling me it proves what a good Chief Constable I will make. I've shot myself in the foot, Freeman."

"How does Geoff Mercer feel about leaving London Road?" asked Gus. "I reckon Christine would have reservations."

"I've never told Mercer that I planned to ensure he stayed close to me if I accepted the late boost up the ladder," said Kenneth Truelove. "If I had, he might have dismissed the approach from West Mercia out of hand. If I mention it now, he'll think it's just an eleventh-hour attempt to hold on to him."

"Is Geoff determined to leave?" asked Gus.

"I don't know," said the ACC. "He spends as little time in my office as possible. He confines our conversation to the matter at hand. Mercer dashed off earlier to avoid seeing you."

"I was a few minutes late," said Gus. "I apologised."

"It wouldn't have mattered," said the ACC. "Geoff was itching to leave. He knows that when the two of you get together, he relaxes and he's scared that if you get a sniff of what's going on, you won't let him leave until you worm it out of him."

"He's a friend," said Gus, "not that I ever thought I'd say that. Now I know there's a danger that he'll disappear to another part of the country. I'll say my piece when I catch up with him. He'd be a fool to leave London Road. With you at the helm and Geoff as one of your ACCs, it would have the makings of a dream team."

"I never know when to take you seriously, Freeman. Is this another of your wind-ups?"

"Don't be daft, sir. You've always been a great copper, the archetypal administrator. The role you've tried to avoid is tailor-made for a man of your calibre. The other officers on the same ACC rung of the ladder are dedicated professionals, but they don't have the gravitas you possess. Mercer is the perfect piece of the jigsaw to complete the Wiltshire picture. We need to work together to make sure it happens."

"We agree on something at last," smiled Kenneth Truelove. "It might need work, but I can see a way forward now. Thank you, Freeman. Now, back to business."

"Why am I bothered over the fate of the dogs? It must be old age. According to villagers in Pontyclun that I spoke to, they could be vicious little beggars, yet those puppies adored Lexie Kendall. The more I heard of Lexie's experiences, the more I wanted to do something that brought a smile to her face."

"It might sound lucky, Freeman, but I met a chap at our church the other Sunday. He's the editor of a newspaper. Once a month, we invite people with a heart-warming story to share with our congregation instead of a sermon. When we chatted after morning service, he told me he knew of an investigative reporter who would have more to offer on the subject you mentioned, but he'd never get them to agree to appear in public."

"They work undercover, I take it?" said Gus.

"Quite, and when I pressed him further, he told me they were investigating the widespread incidence of illegal dog fights. This reporter's cover name is Mitch. I have a phone number for the editor. Would you like me to call him to see if he can set up a meeting between the two of you? It sounds as if you could get a better insight into the business from someone who's been at the sharp end."

"It would be a start," said Gus. "After I've met with this Mitch, I need your blessing to attend an interview with Dai Williams. Let's call it a quid pro quo for my help keeping Geoff Mercer on our doorstep."

"You had better hope DI Williams gets the Corbett twins to open up then, Freeman," said the ACC. "I will allow you to travel to Cardiff to sit in on an interview with the accused, but you must tread carefully. Remember what it says on that ID card of yours."

"Consultant, sir," said Gus, "how could I forget."

"I have another cold case here ready for your attention," said the ACC. "Is your team ready to work on it straight away in your absence?"

"My brief meeting with this Mitch person and a half-day in South Wales won't disrupt operations at the Old Police Station office, sir. We can handle it."

"If you think he's up to the job, get DS Hardy to take control while you're off-site," said the ACC.

"Good idea, sir," said Gus. "Right, what am I looking at?"

"It's a departure for the Crime Review Team, Freeman.

So far, the team has only dealt with the murder of adults. This case concerns a thirteen-year-old schoolgirl, Stacey Read, who went missing for ten days before her body turned up in the Wilts & Berks Canal in February 2015. Stacey had been stabbed twice, in the chest and stomach, before drowning in the water. Her body was partially clothed. Swindon detectives suspected a sexual motive in her killing. However, despite a high-profile investigation, the case remains unsolved."

"Where in Swindon was this?" asked Gus, "I'm struggling to remember the case."

"You had other things on your mind, Freeman. You were coming to terms with your wife's death. It's no surprise that this case has slipped your memory. The Wilts & Berks is a canal linking the Kennet & Avon Canal to the Thames at Abingdon. The North Wilts Canal merged with it to become a branch to the Thames and Severn Canal near Cricklade."

"Surely, far too much of those old waterways have dried up or got built over to get resurrected?"

"You might think so, but experts believe we'll get forced back to the water when the fossil fuels run out. A living, breathing canal through the middle of several towns would boost tourism and do wonders for the local economy."

"Do these dreamers remember who dug those trenches in the first place? Fat chance of getting several thousand Irish navvies over to rectify the damage."

"That's as may be, Freeman," said the ACC. "they found the body at a place called Rushey Platt. It's a wooded area with a nature reserve and a stretch of the old canal. The nearest main road is the A3102, which connects Swindon to Royal Wootton Bassett."

"Okay, I'm getting my bearings now," said Gus. "Where did the victim live?"

"Stacey lived with her mother, Debbie, and younger sister, Lucy, off Chapel Street, Gorse Hill."

"How far is that from where they found the body?" asked Gus.

"Three miles, a ten-minute drive," said Kenneth Truelove.

"Stacey was stabbed twice and drowned. Was she dead before she went into the water? Did the detectives at Gablecross determine whether the murder occurred at Rushey Platt, or did the initial attack occur elsewhere? Do we have that information?"

"The evidence pointed to everything having taken place at Rushey Platt," said the ACC. "I'm sure you'll find the details you want in the murder file."

"Anything significant on the family unit?" asked Gus. "You didn't mention a father living at the address in Gorse Hill. Was the family known to the police?"

"Stacey and Lucy often stayed overnight with close relatives. Debbie has a sister who lives in Penhill, two streets across from Stacey's grandmother. They're named Vanessa Nicholls and Mary Bennett. On Sunday, the eighth of February, the last day that friends and family saw Stacey, the two girls spent the day at their grandmother's house in Penhill. At around six in the evening, Stacey took her eleven-year-old sister back to the family home off Chapel Street. There didn't appear to be any cause for concern. Debbie said Stacey was her normal sensible self and reminded her mother to leave the bus fare on the kitchen table in the morning for the girls to get to school the next day."

"Did Gablecross check with the school or neighbours

whether Stacey was as level-headed or sensible as her mother claimed?" asked Gus.

"They did, and in the weeks leading up to her death, Stacey played truant. She was street-smart for a thirteen-year-old and preferred to hang out with friends on the nearby estate. When she left home on Sunday evening at seven, Debbie thought Stacey stayed the night at her sister Vanessa's house. Stacey never arrived at the house in Penhill, and she didn't turn up for school the next morning."

"When did her mother report her missing?" asked Gus.

"On Wednesday morning," said the ACC. "As soon as she returned from work that evening, Debbie started looking for Stacey herself. She didn't think the officer she spoke with took the matter seriously."

"Was that because the officer knew the family?" asked Gus. "If Stacey mixed with the wrong sort on the nearby estate, he could have thought that going missing for a few days wasn't unusual behaviour."

"We can't know what Stacey got up to, but the family had never been in trouble with the law. However, one witness that Debbie Read discovered said she saw Stacey arguing with a lad near the allotments near Redpost Drive."

"I think I've driven past that allotment site," said Gus. "It's huge compared to the one at Urchfont. A large family pub nearby, too, that got refurbished around five years ago. They make an excellent Sunday lunch. How far was that sighting from where the murder took place?"

"If Stacey and her killer accessed the nature reserve from Redpost Drive, it's half a mile from the main road."

"The argument could have been unrelated," said Gus. "Her body lay in the canal until Wednesday the eighteenth, am I right?"

"That's correct," said the ACC. "The autopsy confirmed that Stacey's body had been in the water for over a week. Detectives proceeded with their investigation, assuming that the murder took place on Sunday evening. There were no confirmed sightings of Stacey after the one that Debbie found."

"Do we have a record of the time when Stacey argued with the boy?" asked Gus.

"Between seven-thirty and eight," said the ACC.

"How did she get there? Her mother confirmed that she left home around seven o'clock. It would take far longer than that to walk that distance. Stacey must have caught a bus, or someone picked her up in a car. Was there any hint of an older boyfriend?"

"Swindon has excellent public transport," said Kenneth Truelove, "Stacey could have travelled between her home and Redpost Drive on a Sunday evening. The witness didn't mention a car being in the vicinity. The youngster arguing with Stacey was around her age, according to Debbie. There's nothing in the murder file concerning boyfriends of any age."

"It's not going well, is it?" sighed Gus. "What persuaded Stacey to change her mind about staying with her Aunt Vanessa? The story so far suggests it wasn't unusual for Stacey to stay overnight with her. We'll learn why that was later. I must speak to Vanessa Nicholls to confirm, but if Debbie was happy for Stacey to leave home at seven on a cold February evening, she expected she'd go straight to Vanessa's house."

"Penhill is in the opposite direction to Rushey Platt," said the ACC, "and Stacey could get there in fifteen minutes if she hopped on a bus."

"What was the witness doing at that time?" asked Gus.

"The usual, walking the dog," said the ACC. "The lady was on the other side of the road and saw two kids aged thirteen and fifteen arguing under a street lamp."

"How did she know it was Stacey? Did she recognise her?"

"Debbie Read told police that the witness had a son and daughter who attended the same school. Debbie described Stacey's clothing when she left home, and the woman said that it matched what she'd seen."

"Two kids wrapped up in hoodies, jeans, gloves, scarf and trainers," said Gus. "From the other side of the road, I'd be hard-pressed to tell if it was two lads or two girls. Could the dog-walker hear the argument? Could she tell Debbie what it was about?"

"Traffic was light on the road and the pavements. The cold weather kept most people indoors. Although she couldn't tell Debbie what was said, she was adamant the girl was Stacey, and it was a boy she was arguing with."

"Did Stacey have a mobile phone?" asked Gus.

"Debbie Read told detectives that Stacey got a pay-as-you-go mobile for her thirteenth birthday. She had it with her when she left home. There was no reason to check her whereabouts on Sunday evening. Debbie left for work at seven in the morning. Lucy took the cash from the kitchen table for the bus fares and sweets. When Debbie got home in the early evening, and there was no sign of her eldest daughter, she asked Lucy if she'd seen her. Lucy told her mother it wasn't unusual to miss one another at a school with sixteen hundred pupils. Debbie couldn't contact Stacey on her phone. She assumed Stacey switched it off or forgot to take a charger to Vanessa's house."

"Did Debbie call her sister?" asked Gus.

"Not on Monday night. She kept ringing Stacey's

phone. On Tuesday evening, when Lucy was home again, Debbie called Vanessa. That was the first time Debbie learned Stacey hadn't spent the night in Penhill with her sister."

"Why didn't they call the police straight away?" asked Gus.

"Remember where Stacey and Lucy had spent most of Sunday," said the ACC. "They visited Mary Bennett, their grandmother. Vanessa suggested that Stacey had changed her mind and stayed with her Gran instead. Mrs Bennett didn't own a mobile, so Debbie called her landline but got no reply. Vanessa agreed to walk across the estate to their mother's house to check she was alright and see whether Stacey was there. At around ten in the evening, Vanessa called Debbie to say that Mary had just got home from playing bingo in Greenbridge. Mary hadn't seen Stacey since she left with Lucy on Sunday afternoon. Debbie called into the police station on Wednesday morning on her way to work."

"Was Stacey's mobile recovered at the scene?" asked Gus.

"Divers explored the canal, and officers carried out a fingertip search of the undergrowth in the area without luck."

"The killer may have taken it with them and disposed of it," said Gus. "That could prove significant. The phone must have contained incriminating information. Otherwise, why bother?"

"You think the absence of the phone suggests the killer wasn't a stranger," said the ACC. "What if Stacey lost it in a struggle? We've not ruled out the possibility that Stacey arrived in Rushey Platt by car or that an older man was responsible for her not reaching her aunt's house. Someone could have seen Stacey at Gorse Hill South, waiting at the bus stop, offered her a lift, and driven out to Rushey Platt."

"Someone drove her to a secluded spot to carry out a sexual assault," said Gus. "He tries it on in the car first, and that's where Stacey and the mobile part company. Matters turn ugly, and when they're in the nature reserve, he stabs Stacey and dumps her body in the canal. That doesn't sound far-fetched, but the eyewitness was adamant Stacey was under that street lamp, half a mile away, arguing with a young lad thirty minutes after leaving home. She could have accepted a lift from someone she knew. We could ask the family if Stacey would have gone willingly with a friend of the family or neighbour. No doubt, Debbie warned both girls of the dangers of accepting lifts from strangers."

"If the witness statement is unshakeable," said the ACC, "then the killer was that young lad or someone who arrived on the scene after the witness walked off with her dog."

"At this stage, we can't even rule out there being more than one attacker," said Gus. "This case has a strange feel to it. We have a family that doesn't appear to have an adult male presence. Debbie's children spent long periods away from home with their aunt or grandmother. Their mother left for work at seven o'clock every day. Where did she work?"

"Debbie worked for Royal Mail out at the Dorcan Mail Centre," said the ACC. "She cycled to work, just under thirty minutes each way. Her shift was from seven-thirty to three-thirty. The girls' father, Pat, worked at the Honda factory. He left Debbie in 2007 when Stacey was six years old. Pat Read did not try to get custody or have the girls at weekends or holidays."

"He just abandoned his family and didn't look back,"

said Gus. "What a charmer. Were his maintenance payments up to date?"

"They were never an issue, according to the report in the file. Honda deducted the money from Read's salary and paid it to Debbie. The financial transaction was the only link between them."

"So, Stacey hadn't been in contact with her father behind her mother's back?" asked Gus, "It wasn't Pat Read that stopped to pick her up from the bus stop? Where does he live?"

"Moredon Road," said the ACC. "Pat Read has a fifteen-minute drive to work every day in his Honda."

"What about the grandmother?"

"Widowed in 2006," said the ACC, "Harry died of lung cancer, aged sixty-nine. Before you ask, Vanessa's husband, Barry, was a long-distance lorry driver who spent so much time on the continent he moved to Germany a decade ago to live with a barmaid called Helga. They live in Dusseldorf with one child and three Alsatians. Barry and Vanessa didn't have any children before the split."

"For once, we can't fault the detail that the detectives at Gablecross went into on their first run at this case. We've got plenty of names to pursue to arrange interviews. I don't envisage Barry Nicholls offering much help, though. Is there anything else you think warrants a highlight before I drive back to brief the team, sir?"

"I don't know whether it helps or hinders, Freeman," said the ACC. "Jack Sanders was SIO on this case. No big surprise with it being the murder of a child. Jack gave an interview to the media where he stated he believed Stacey went to the nature reserve with a group of people she knew, and to use his actual phrase—things progressed far more than they expected. It was Jack who thought there was a sexual motive. Police found items of Stacey's clothing in two separate areas of the canal bank nearby. There was no post-mortem evidence of a sexual assault. At the inquest in June 2015, the coroner said Stacey might have drowned trying to escape her attacker or attackers. It appeared they had undressed her under threat. Although there was no evidence of sexual assault, the killer may have intended to molest or rape her. Stacey got shoved into the canal after the stabbing or went into the water to escape, and the stabbing took place there. It was February, and the water was freezing; the cause of death was drowning. The coroner returned a verdict of unlawful killing."

"Police found clothing in two distinct areas," said Gus, "that ties in with the theory that her attacker wanted to rape her, but Stacey got away during his first attempt. The notion of several males in the nature reserve that night terrorising a thirteen-year-old girl is abhorrent. Stacey could easily have slipped into the water as she ran, partially clothed, along the canal bank, trying to escape in the dark. What conclusions did the detectives draw regarding the stab wounds?"

"A five-inch blade made both wounds," said the ACC. "It was impossible to tell whether the same weapon made them. Stacey's body had been in the water for over a week, and Rushey Platt is a nature reserve."

"There was plenty of vermin present apart from the two-legged variety on Sunday, the eighth of February," said Gus.

"Quite," said Kenneth Truelove.

Chapter Four

GUS GATHERED the contents of the Stacey Read murder file and slipped them back into the folder. Time to head for the Old Police Station office and start work.

He left the ACC gazing out of his window and braved the walk to the top of the stairs.

"Mr Freeman, how can you run off without saying hello?"

"Good morning, Kassie. No, it's past twelve o'clock. Good afternoon."

"I'd already showed Mr Mercer and the ACC my muffins before you arrived today."

"The team had work to complete for Mr Truelove, Kassie," said Gus. "He kindly delayed our meeting until eleven. Although, I managed to arrive late for that, as I expect you noticed."

"I was still wheeling my trolley around, Mr Freeman, but Vera mentioned the mini-wave and the watch."

"How is Ms Butler?" asked Gus.

"Hark at you, Ms Butler, indeed. Vera is at lunch. I have

to take my break when she returns today. Mr Mercer delegated tasks to DI Packenham. She's new and upsetting Status Quo, or that's what your Suzie said. I call it changing for change's sake. If it isn't broken, why mess with it?"

"My thoughts exactly. Kassie," said Gus. "Where did this latest DI spring from?"

"Grace," said Kassie making the name last far more than a heartbeat, "came from Portishead."

"I'll get the details from Suzie tonight," said Gus.

"You'll interrogate her, I suppose," said Kassie with a grin. "Is it still roses around the door in Urchfont?"

"Early days," said Gus, "and early nights too. There are no storm clouds on the horizon, Kassie. You can stop trying to turn back the clock."

"Alright for some," groaned the loveless Kassie Trotter. Gus thought he saw the opportunity to escape. He took one step towards the ground floor.

"Don't you dare," said Kassie. "I've got something I want you to sample. I have given no one else a slice of this yet."

"Another busy weekend baking then," said Gus.

"I've been practising for next month," said Kassie.

Gus returned to the mezzanine and waited while Kassie retrieved an item wrapped in tinfoil from one of her Tupperware boxes.

"Try this with your afternoon coffee," she said, "and let me know what you think."

"Can I ask what it is?" asked Gus.

"A Welsh tea bread," said Kassie, "they call it bara brith, or speckled bread. It should have butter spread on it like a malt loaf, but I don't suppose you stock that in the office."

"I'm sure I'll get the idea, Kassie," said Gus. "This package feels like you've given me a sizeable portion."

"I never let my gentleman friends go short," she said as she shuffled back to her desk.

Gus headed to the car park, wondering whether Rhys Evans, the new Police Surgeon, had any idea what lay in wait for him.

When Gus exited the lift and entered the CRT office, he found five eager team members poised to hear their next case.

"I hope you found something useful to occupy the two hours I've been away?"

"I did," said Blessing Umeh. The others looked at her.

"Good," said Gus. "The ACC has handed us an unsolved case from 2015. Someone stabbed a teenage girl from Swindon and dumped her body in the canal."

"Stacey," said DS Neil Davis.

"You remember the case, Neil?"

"Yes, guv. Colonel Sanders took charge of that one. He oversaw the Burnside case from May until around the end of the year. Jack was coming up to retirement age and thought that was his swansong. Then Stacey…"

"Read," said Gus.

"That was it, Stacey Read. Her death got ruled an unlawful killing, didn't it? Jake Latimer told me the Colonel couldn't find a suspect, no matter how hard he tried. Jack Sanders always found it tough dealing with cases involving children."

"Who doesn't, Neil," said DS Luke Sherman.

Gus knew what both Neil and Luke meant.

It was impossible not to get affected by the unlawful death of a child. Jack Sanders also found it challenging to deal with the girls that survived the grooming scandal. Gus wondered whether something in Jack's past lay behind that exaggerated concern.

"I'll let you have access to the murder file in a few minutes," said Gus. "I want to tell you what I'll be doing over the next few days. I won't be in tomorrow morning. The ACC will call me later this afternoon to let me know where I can meet an investigative reporter working under-cover on the dogfighting circuit."

"Is that this side of the Severn Bridge, or in South Wales, guv?" asked Luke.

"In the West Country, Luke, I'm afraid. I'll be back before lunch, and then I'm returning to Cardiff Central in the afternoon or the following morning."

"Armed with knowledge about dogs similar to the ones that Lexie Kendall exercised," said Neil. "Are you going to interview the Corbett brothers, guv?"

"I can't, Neil," said Gus. "The ACC has agreed that I can brief Dai Williams and sit in on his interview. Dai Williams will get as many answers as he can. I'll decide what to do next after conversing with Dai."

"Is that within our remit, guv?" asked DS Alex Hardy.

"No, Alex," said Gus. "Neil and Luke thought persuading Lexie to get reacquainted with her mother was the right thing to do. However, I feel we need to go the extra mile in this area of the case too."

"Anything else, guv?" asked Lydia Logan Barre.

"While I'm away, Alex will be in charge. I know it might mean the CRT office is without a chief for only eight to ten hours, but the ACC wants us to operate at maximum effi-ciency at all times."

"Fair enough, guv," said Neil. "Luke and I can sub for you whenever the occasion arises."

Gus caught Lydia's sidelong look at DC Blessing Umeh. He had three Detective Sergeants on the team. Gus hadn't considered which of them was the senior officer. Alex was the eldest, and Neil had a good deal of experience. Luke was the only team member with proven firearm skills. But, of course, Blessing was a junior member as a mere Detective Constable.

Where did that leave Lydia? She was the ACC's graduate intake and slipped into the Crime Review Team within months of leaving university. Although a civilian, Gus had unconsciously set Lydia on par with the guys. He would need to share the captain's armband with the first four team members in the room. Gus shook his head. Why did he listen to that Geoff Mercer and agree to come out of retirement? He made a mental note to give Geoff a ring. Maybe they should meet for a pint after he'd paid his visit to Cardiff.

"Right, let's get this murder file split up," said Gus. "We need maps of Swindon and crime scene photos on the wallboards, please. Luke, you can prepare a list of potential interviewees. Neil, can you hunt down maps and the history of the Wilts & Berks and Kennet & Avon Canals?"

"That's easy, guv," said Neil, "I studied canals at school. Unfortunately, the fifty-two-mile canal that opened in 1810 was abandoned by the start of WWI–a fate hastened by the collapse of the Stanley aqueduct at the turn of the century. Much of the canal subsequently became unnavigable. Army demolition exercises in WWII damaged many of the structures, and since then, parts of the route got filled in, or housing estates covered the ground they occupied. Around forty years ago, local people set up a group that aimed to restore the canal fully. The group has restored several locks and bridges and re-watered over eight miles of the canal."

"You must dig out the maps, Neil," said Gus. "I remember the Queen opening something near Devizes thirty years ago, but I can't see how that connects yet with the stretch of canal at Rushey Platt."

"Is it relevant, guv?" asked Blessing Umeh. "I've skipped through the initial summary of the case, and Stacey Read's body was in a secluded part of an old canal. Her killer had to be local, surely?"

"I've lived around here longer than you, Blessing," said Gus. "Canoeists have competed in an annual race from Devizes to Westminster for years, and long stretches of the canal network see cyclists tearing along the towpath. As Neil pointed out, dotted here and there are navigable stretches. Until I can rule out the possibility someone other than a local was near that stretch of water on the night of the attack, I'll keep every option open."

"Fair enough, guv," said Blessing.

Neil Davis walked past Blessing's desk fifteen minutes later with items to pin on a wallboard beside her.

"Anyone would be mad to canoe or cycle at eight or nine o'clock at night in February, Blessing," he said. "But if the canal was navigable enough to allow a barge to reach that spot and it moored there overnight, there is a chance Stacey bumped into a stranger. It doesn't gel with the idea that she went there with a gang of people that the coroner's report suggested, though."

"Oh, I haven't got to that bit yet, Neil. What were your first impressions?"

"I don't think it was the young lad. He might carry a knife like many others his age, but an eyewitness saw him and Stacey arguing. So why would Stacey walk half a mile in the dark to that nature reserve with someone she'd just argued with?"

"Perhaps he chased Stacey, and where the attack took

place was random. Did Stacey even know the nature reserve? Did she realise she was running into danger?"

Neil shook his head.

"Let's assume he chased Stacey, caught her and stabbed her as he tried to rip off her top. In the struggle, Stacey ended up in the water. What would a boy of fourteen or fifteen do in that situation?"

"Panic," said Blessing.

"Despite an exhaustive search, the police never found Stacey's phone," said Neil. "Yet her key ring, loose change, and handkerchief were in a purse in her jacket pocket. The phone would incriminate her killer, so they took it with them. That's cold. Not something I associate with a young lad's reactions to such an awful incident."

"You said that the verdict was death by drowning," said Blessing. "Would the poor girl have died from the stab wounds?"

"If she received prompt treatment, then it sounds as if she could have survived, but we can't know what happened from the evidence we have in the file. There was bruising, but no blunt force trauma recorded, so they didn't knock her out, but they could have forced her into the canal and stabbed her."

"How awful," said Blessing, "I wonder why she couldn't get back out?"

Neil looked at the crime scene photos and wondered the same thing.

The ACC called Gus at half-past four to tell him where and when to meet Mitch. Gus was off to the county town in the morning. He looked at the clock: it had been a long day.

"Find a convenient point to stop and call it a day," he said. "I'll see you after eleven in the morning."

Gus switched off his computer and walked to the lift.

He heard the rustle of papers and the scraping of chairs. The team wouldn't be far behind him.

As he drove home to Urchfont, he considered their new case. How could they identify that young lad seen arguing with Stacey? He was vital to everything that followed that argument. Either he went with Stacey, or their row caused her to go off with someone else. No matter how Gus tried to make the pieces of the jigsaw fit, he failed. It was hopeless until they discovered what caused Stacey Read to go to Rushey Platt rather than her aunt's home.

Gus swung the Focus into the gateway and parked next to Suzie.

"I'm home," he called as he stepped into the hallway.

"I've prepared a salad this evening. I hope you don't mind."

Suzie appeared from the bedroom. Her hair was loose on her shoulders.

"Just changed from your uniform?" asked Gus.

"I got in twenty minutes ago, went straight to the kitchen, and then changed. What sort of day have you had?"

Gus told her the news on the Kendall case and that the team was investigating the 2015 murder of Stacey Read.

"I'm meeting someone in Trowbridge in the morning," he said, "background on the dogfighting circuit. Then, I'll drive to Cardiff. Dai Williams is still interviewing the Corbett twins."

"I assume you'll be sitting in the corner trying not to jump in with questions," said Suzie.

"Kenneth Truelove gave his permission as long as I don't take part in proceedings," said Gus. "After our chat, Kassie told me you'd got a new companion."

"Grace Packenham?" said Suzie with a grimace. "She

arrived this morning and has already put half a dozen people's noses out of joint. I know it's usual to be seen to be doing something when you start a new job, but it pays to check the lay of the land before blundering in like a bull in a china shop."

"She's certainly sparked an avalanche of cliches," said Gus. "Was the PCC responsible for her appointment? Did she replace Gareth Francis?"

"I can never work out what those at the top think, Gus. Since Geoff Mercer handed me my latest project, he left me to my own devices. That suits me. I grasp what they want from it, but I'd prefer to check in with my immediate superior now and then. Geoff disappeared on a course, and he's hardly spoken since he got back."

"Are there any rumours flying around?" asked Gus.

"Have you heard anything?" Suzie asked.

"The ACC reckons West Mercia wants Geoff. He was the star of the show at that course you mentioned."

"A promotion? It doesn't explain why he's so distant from everyone at London Road. Geoff's one of us, part of the furniture. I would expect him to say he's not interested. Do you think Geoff's giving it serious consideration? Is that why he's keeping us at arm's length? He's preparing to leave the family."

"I hope not," said Gus. "The ACC wants me to check with Geoff, see what he has in mind, and then persuade him to stay. I plan to get him to meet me for a pint one evening this week."

"Perhaps, I should come too," said Suzie. "I'll hold him while you knock sense into him."

"I thought I'd try the subtle approach," said Gus.

"Off you go and get changed. I'll put the finishing touches to this meal."

"Pour us a glass of something cool," said Gus, "we'll eat outside in the back garden. Take advantage of the warm evening sun."

"We've got a Sauvignon Blanc in the fridge," said Suzie.

"That will be cool," said Gus. He went to the bedroom to change.

Tuesday, 17 July 2018

"I THINK last night was the first time that I've used that garden furniture since Tess died," said Gus as he and Suzie ate breakfast.

"I remember falling into it when I was drunk that afternoon," said Suzie.

"The day you swore undying love to me," said Gus. "I should have kept the security film of that event to play to you. It cost an arm and a leg to get those cameras installed. They seemed a good idea at the time, but thank goodness, things have quietened down since then."

"The furniture looked care-worn last night," said Suzie. "I might buy a tin of wood stain at the weekend and freshen it up."

"Or we could take it to the recycling centre and buy a new set?" said Gus. "It would be ours then."

"What do you want to do tonight?" asked Suzie. "If you have to drive to Cardiff, I imagine you could be back late?"

"We'll stick to our usual routine," said Gus. "If I'm late, we'll go directly to the Lamb for a meal. If I'm home from the office at half-past five, we'll visit the pub after spending an hour on the allotment."

"I'll expect you when I see you then," said Suzie as she headed for the shower.

After Suzie left for work at London Road, Gus showered and dressed. His appointment was at ten. Gus drove into Trowbridge and parked the car in a multi-storey car park.

The place didn't look great, but who would hot-wire a clapped-out Ford Focus? It was worth the risk. Gus made his way into the nearby courtyard and entered the café.

There were several elderly couples, and single mums sat sour-faced at tables. It was par for the course. A woman in the far corner lifted her head, suggesting he came to join her. Could that be Mitch? Or was she just lonely?

A staff member behind the counter looked up from the book she was reading.

"Can I get you something?" she asked with what passed for a smile.

The effort must have tired her because she didn't look ready to spring into action just yet.

"A black coffee, without, please," said Gus.

"You had better tell her that meant without sugar, not without a cup," said the woman at the corner table as Gus reached her.

"Mitch?" asked Gus.

"That's me. I never liked Michelle. Sit yourself down. You're drawing attention. Not good in my line of work."

"I heard you could tell me about blood sports in the region," whispered Gus.

"Black, without. Don't you want a Danish pastry? They're on special offer."

It was Smiler.

"I have to watch my waistline," said Gus.

The girl tutted.

"Please yourself."

"Drink it while it's still tepid," said Mitch. "My editor said you wanted background. Take notes, but don't record this conversation."

"Not taking any chances, are you?" said Gus, taking a notepad from his jacket pocket.

"I've worked undercover in six counties across the south of England. You don't see many women at events on the fighting circuit. My editor warned me how bad it could get, but nothing prepares you for the reality. I wanted to tell readers what was happening under their noses, even if it meant rubbing shoulders with the dregs of society."

"I have no idea how tough it was to watch, knowing that if they saw you cared for the animals, it could end badly for you."

Mitch took a file from the large handbag on the seat beside her.

"This is part of the article I wrote after my first month undercover," she said. "Men gather around as their chosen fighter tears flesh from its opponent. You would think this was a tale from yesteryear, but it's this year, and dog fights are taking place in empty buildings, parks, and back yards across the country. If you have the depraved mind that enjoys the spectacle, you can find a fight somewhere, every day of the year."

"How long ago was the blood sport outlawed?" asked Gus.

"Two hundred years ago," said Mitch. "Despite the ban, the RSPCA receives over five thousand reports yearly of organised fights. Only five percent of those reports result in a conviction."

"And they say the police clear-up rate is poor," said Gus. "What could I expect to pay for a fighting dog?"

"At least a grand these days. Although, you don't look

like someone that would spend that amount of money if you knew the misery these animals endure from the day they're born until the moment they get killed. I could take you to a field less than five miles from here where I found three mutilated dogs just chucked under the hedgerow."

"Where did you find most of these fights were taking place?" asked Gus. He finished his coffee. Mitch was right.

"Wherever you've got a housing estate populated with young men with gang connections. They're home all day, and time drags. One way to fill the idle hours is an impromptu scrap between dogs from strong breeds, such as the pit bull or Staffordshire terrier. Why do they have the dogs tethered on a chain outside their property in the first place? Sometimes it's for protection. It's often a status symbol, like tattoos, jewellery, and clothing. The owners release the dogs in the back yard or alleyway at street level, the nearby park, and have a few minutes of sport. Education's a wonderful thing. A pity so many young men of that ilk spent much of their school life excluded."

"I take it you observed this behaviour from a discreet distance?"

"There's not enough make-up in Hollywood to get me into that scene," said Mitch. "I worked in a burger van that cruised the estates. The driver shut up shop after the lunchtime trade and left me in the back. I had spy holes on both sides of the van to check what was happening."

"Can you tell me which town you were in?" asked Gus.

"Swindon," said Mitch, "there's no point telling you which estate. It happens everywhere."

"What about organised events? How did you get access to those?"

"There's a circuit that operates in every region across the country. That's when the organisers use an abandoned building or warehouse. Gang members go with friends and acquaintances. That was my way in, hanging around the pubs they use, getting into conversations over a pool table or on a fruit machine. The organisers set up a pit with tyres or wooden pallets to keep the fight enclosed. The crowd gathers around the pit, the betting starts, and the dogs are let loose."

"How long do these fights last?" asked Gus.

"It varies in these unregulated fights. It can be over in minutes, but there's another level I've not been able to access so far. As long ago as 2006, the League Against Cruel Sports found evidence of a highly organised covert operation staging professional fights. They have referees, rules, and timekeepers. I've heard that fights between matched dogs can last several hours."

"Prosecuting far more owners involved in the five thousand reported fights would help," said Gus. Mitch shook her head.

"Not much. The maximum sentence for cases heard in Magistrates Courts is only twelve months. The maximum fine has risen from five to twenty thousand pounds. In Crown Courts, where more serious cases get heard, the maximum sentence for animal cruelty has increased from two to five years. So few cases ever get that far."

"One in four people in the UK own a dog," said Gus. "Most treat them as part of the family. The thought of a dog getting brutalised, beaten, and forced into a fight to the death is the stuff of nightmares."

"We should leave," said Mitch, "your friend behind the counter keeps giving us dirty looks."

"I'll settle the bill," said Gus. "Thanks for the insight. I don't envy you having to follow this murky business."

"It's a living," grunted Mitch as she stood up from her chair.

Gus crossed to the counter and paid for his coffee and Mitch's breakfast order. Smiler committed the ultimate sin and hoped he 'had a nice day' as she dropped his change into his hand. Gus promised himself he wouldn't be back.

When he turned around, he found that Mitch had already disappeared.

As he crossed the road to return to the car park, he wondered whether there wasn't another way to put his mind at rest. When he got back to the office, he called Dai Williams.

DAI WILLIAMS WAS UNAVAILABLE. They were still in the interview room. The officer who took the call promised to relay the message to Gus when DI Williams was free.

"Anything to report, Alex," said Gus.

"We've completed posting the maps and wallboards, guv. Luke's got a list of people he thought we should interview first. Please take a look and add any others you think we've missed. Neil's done some digging on the Kennet & Avon."

"I told you it would be tough to find those Irish navvies, Neil," said Gus.

"Very droll, guv," said Neil. "A Trust started work on restoring the canal from Reading to Bristol in the early Sixties. They thought it could be a valuable public amenity. You were right that the Queen paid a visit to Devizes. In 1990, she opened the refurbished Caen Hill locks, where twenty-nine locks raise the boats' level by two-hundred and thirty-seven feet in two miles. But the Wilts & Berks Canal ran into the centre of Swindon. So the volunteers involved have worked at places like Moredon to refurbish the aqueduct. If you look at their website, you will see that things have moved on since the murder. They have a canal boat named 'Dragonfly' with two crew and room for a dozen passengers. Trips usually run from a landing stage at Wichelstowe to Kingshill and back, lasting approximately fifty minutes. Public trips now run, weather permitting, every weekend & Bank Holiday through the year, plus Wednesdays during the school holidays."

"That's all very well, Neil, but was that stretch navigable at the time of the murder?"

"It was, guv," said Neil. "Bear with me. There's more on the nature reserve and the canal in this article I researched. When the canal opened for trade transport, Swindon was a small market town still based on the hill now referred to as Old Town, and to keep the ten-mile long canal topped up with fresh water; they created Coate Water, which is now a country park on the eastern edge of town. As we know, the narrowboat trade was rendered obsolete with steam, and the canal was abandoned at the start of WWI. Much of its route got filled in and built over. Still, the stretch between Kingshill Road and the Wichelstowe development park survives. It's now a popular destination for bird watchers, dog walkers, and families with kids searching for tadpoles, not to mention families of swans and mallard ducks. The Rushey Platt nature reserve, which Wiltshire Wildlife Trust manages, is halfway along the canal. The wild space is a remnant of the lush wetland marsh that covered much of south Swindon before land drainage made this habitat uncommon in Wiltshire. Wildlife is vital, sandwiched between the River Ray, Wilts and Berks Canal and the former Old Town railway line. That last stretch of the canal is at the heart of the Canalside development, which will see new homes spring up alongside the canal footpaths. Even in February 2015, a boat could leave the landing stage at Wichelstowe to navigate the waterway as far as Kingshill Road."

"How far is Kingshill Road from Redpost Drive, where the eyewitness saw Stacy arguing with the lad?" asked Gus.

"Half a mile, guv," said Neil.

"So, a boat *could* have been on that stretch of the canal that night," said Gus. "Even if the 'Dragonfly' wasn't operating then. When did it start, by the way?"

"Camilla, the Duchess of Cornwall, opened the regenerated landing stage in 2017, guv," said Neil, "I remember seeing it on the TV. It was chucking it with rain. They wheeled in Camilla to name the 'Dragonfly' too, but that must have been six or seven years earlier."

"That naming ceremony was in 2010, guv," said Luke. "They got the boat to celebrate the two hundredth anniversary of the original canal opening. Trips have taken place since 2010."

"There you are, Blessing," said Gus. "I'm not sure how you get a boat, a coracle, or a kayak onto a stretch of water without anyone noticing. But even if that landing stage needed remedial work in 2015, we've got another possibility to pursue."

"I'm not sure it helps," said Blessing. "If it was the young lad on Redpost Drive, we have half a chance of identifying him. Following up on Stacey's school friends and local teenagers who frequented the nature reserve would also take time, but it would be achievable. Where would we even start if we're looking for a mystery man?"

Chapter Five

GUS DROVE HOME at the end of a frustrating day and pondered Blessing Umeh's comment.

He knew the odds were stacked against a craft of any type being on that canal at the time of Stacey's murder. Yet, he couldn't let it go.

Was it one of his inklings again? He needed to visit Redpost Drive and walk the route Stacey must have taken. The crime scene photographs gave them the basic information, but they couldn't substitute for soaking up the essence of the murder site by walking it. Boots on the ground always offered a clearer vision of what took place.

Suzie stood by her car as Gus drove through the gateway. He'd received a call from Dai Williams just after four, inviting him to attend an interview in the morning; he needed to make an early start. Once Gus knew he could get home at a reasonable time, he called Suzie at London Road.

"Give me five minutes to change into my gardening clothes," said Gus, kissing Suzie.

"We've got a good evening for it," she said. "If you're off to Cardiff first thing, you need an early night."

"Yes, miss," said Gus, dashing indoors.

He reappeared in a short-sleeved shirt and jeans. Suzie grabbed his arm, and they made for the allotments.

"Why don't you ever wear shorts," she asked.

"I don't possess any," he replied. "Tess said my legs should remain covered. I never asked why unless I learned something unpleasant about them. I felt it better not to know."

"What have you got lined up for us to tackle this evening," asked Suzie.

"While I'm lifting our potatoes, you can pick a helping of runner beans. I'll check my onions too. In a month from now, the tops will fall over."

"Is that bad?" she asked.

"No, it means the bulbs have stopped swelling. Then we can dry them, string them up, and store them in the shed. They'll be fine for next Spring."

"Where is everyone? There's no sign of Bert or Clemency."

"It's not six o'clock yet," said Gus. "The Reverend might turn up soon. Bert must have worked on his patch this afternoon. The evidence is there before your very eyes, Detective Inspector."

"Bert's harvested beetroot, lettuce and radishes," said Suzie. "The ground in the rows nearest to the remaining plants is freshly hoed. Bert did a spot of watering too. The level in his water butt is lower than when we had our picnic here at the weekend. We haven't had any rain. How did I do?"

"You missed one thing. Bert spotted a touch of potato blight among his crops. He's taken several infected plants away and put them by his shed, ready to burn. They're no good for composting. Unfortunately, that won't kill the disease, and you will get the same problem next year."

"Nobody loves a smartass," said Suzie. "Bert's been and gone then."

The couple had been working for fifteen minutes when Clemency Bentham arrived on her bicycle.

"Evening all," she cried. "Will you be in the Lamb later?"

"I can't see why not," said Gus. "We thought we'd have a meal after we'd finished here."

"Brett said he's around tonight. I thought I'd pop in to keep him company. Bert's watching a programme on TV about bees."

"Would you have to get someone else to read the Banns," Gus asked. "I know little about church etiquette."

The Reverend blushed.

"You are awful, Gus Freeman," she said, "We hardly know one another."

"He's incorrigible, Clemency," said Suzie. "When you left your bicycle at the bungalow last week, Gus couldn't go to bed until he was certain you'd collected it."

"Brett walked me to the bungalow, and I walked with him to Bert's house, if you must know. Then, I wished him good night and cycled home to the rectory. I'm sorry to disappoint."

"How's Irene North?" asked Suzie.

"Irene's over the hangovers from her latest experiment," said Clemency. "That's why Brett said he'd be in the Lamb for an hour or two tonight. Irene's at Bert's studying the bees."

"It could be a double wedding, I suppose," said Gus.

"Now, now, Gus," said Clemency, "if you persist, I must

ask when you two are thinking of getting married. It's a small village, and I've already heard whispers from my parishioners concerning the deplorable increase in the number of couples living in sin."

"We're happy as we are, for now," said Suzie.

"So am I," said the Reverend, "although there is something wrong with my potatoes."

"You had better tell Brett that tonight," said Gus. "Get him to ask his grandfather to spray your crop with the solution he uses. Don't worry, Bert uses nothing harmful to the environment."

"Thanks, Gus," said Clemency. "Now, I must get on. I can see you two have plenty to keep you occupied. Perhaps, I'll catch up with you later?"

Gus nodded. Clemency wasn't staying long. After cycling around the parish this afternoon, she would need to go home to shower and change. Since Brett Penman arrived in the village, the Reverend hadn't entered the Lamb in her gardening clothes. Suzie swore she saw a hint of make-up last week to set off the Laura Ashley, which was a first.

Gus and Suzie completed their chores by seven o'clock, and as he locked their tools away in the shed, he spotted Brett Penman standing in the gateway.

"Hi, Gus, Suzie. Are you coming back later?"

Brett nodded towards the Lamb, just up the lane.

"We've got to make ourselves presentable," said Suzie. "I'm walking over now to book a table. We're returning for a meal whenever they can squeeze us in."

"I'm a third wheel at home tonight," said Brett. "Irene mentioned that she'd brought supper for her and Bert to share after the programme finishes."

"So, you'll be in the Lamb until closing time," said Gus.

"That's my excuse, and I'm sticking to it," laughed Brett.

"The Reverend will keep you company if we get delayed," said Suzie.

This time it was Brett's turn to blush. They walked past the church towards the pub.

"It's impossible to do a thing in a village without everyone knowing, isn't it?"

"You don't need to tell me," said Gus, "I've had to turn the volume up on my TV to mask the tutting from the neighbours."

Brett grinned. He took his mobile phone from his trouser pocket and made a call.

Suzie was heading inside the Lamb when Brett called after her.

"Suzie, can you ask them if they can manage a table for four? Clemency has agreed to join me."

"You exchanged phone numbers last week when you walked home together, then?" asked Gus.

"No, I asked Grandad for Clemency's number last week," said Brett. "That's the first time I've called her, honest. I think she dropped her phone when she realised it was me."

Suzie was soon back in the lane with good news.

"No problem, Brett. They can fit us in at eight o'clock. We'll love you and leave you."

Brett went into the bar, and Gus and Suzie wandered up the lane to the bungalow.

"That's scuppered my chances of an early night," said Gus.

"Not necessarily," said Suzie. "All you need to do is stifle a yawn, and we can leave the love birds in the bar until closing time. You've had a busy day."

"Fair enough," said Gus.

Wednesday, 18 July 2018

GUS LEFT the bungalow at eight o'clock. Suzie was still in the shower.

Last night, after a decent meal and stimulating conversation, Gus had stifled a yawn.

The look Suzie gave him suggested that ten past nine was earlier than she had in mind.

Just before ten, Suzie had stifled a yawn of her own.

"We should get home, as Gus is off to Cardiff first thing," she said. "Thanks for a lovely evening. No doubt we'll see you before the weekend."

They had left Brett and Clemency wedged together on the settle in the corner of the bar.

"They make a delightful couple, don't they?" said Suzie.

"So do we," said Gus as they hurried to the bungalow.

When he fell asleep at half-past twelve, Gus wondered what had happened to the plan for an early night.

GUS KNEW he could make Cardiff Central with minutes to spare if traffic was light before Dai Williams resumed interviewing the Corbett twins. Ninety-five minutes later, he parked his trusty Focus in the visitor's car park and tapped the bonnet to recognise a job well done.

Fingers crossed, it would cope as well with the return trip.

As he negotiated Reception, he spotted a familiar face.

"Good morning, Dai," said Gus, "Any chance of a quick coffee before we get stuck into the interview at ten?"

"I always have a pot brewing in my office, Gus. Come on through once you've got your visitor pass. You know your way by now."

Two minutes later, Gus was enjoying his second black coffee of the day. It wasn't as good as the Gaggia served in the office, but it was good enough.

"I know I needn't remind you, Gus," said Dai Williams. "You're here as an observer."

"I understand, Dai. The brothers and their solicitor would kick up a fuss if a mere consultant started participating in your interview. I've sent you a list of the questions I need answers to. Provided you can slip them in without tipping off the team on the other side of the table, fine. If they get spooked, then back off, and we'll come at it another way. They will ask for frequent comfort breaks if the session lasts for any length. Both brothers smoke. We can use those breaks to reassess our strategy."

"That makes perfect sense," said Dai. "In our earlier interviews, they tried the 'No Comment' approach, but as the evidence we produced became more difficult to deny, they opened up a little."

"How did their brief react to that?" asked Gus.

"We had the usual stops and starts while their brief asked for several minutes to consult with his clients. We weren't letting him delay our progress indefinitely. I called a halt to let Vaughn and Shaun have time to consider. They were more forthcoming in the second session. By yesterday afternoon, the brothers had decided the game was up, and they might as well co-operate as much as they could. This morning we'll learn just how far that co-operation might stretch."

Gus followed Dai Williams and his colleague, DS Annie Morgan, into the interview room.

Vaughn and Shaun Williams entered the room at ten o'clock on the dot, followed by their solicitor. Gus summed him up in one glance. He reminded Gus of Patrick Iverson, the smarmy individual representing the Burnside clan in Swindon.

As DS Morgan breezed through the formalities, Vaughn and Shaun Corbett stared in Gus's direction. The solicitor, a Mr Gerwyn Maddox-Brown, kept his eyes glued to the documents he had taken from his old leather briefcase. Dai Williams didn't allow him to pounce.

"The other person attending this morning is Mr Gus Freeman, a consultant with Wiltshire Police. He's here merely to observe proceedings. South Wales Police are happy that other forces around the country wish to learn from the even-handed way we conduct our interviews with suspects. Mr Freeman may take notes occasionally, but nothing material to this case is permitted. However, I shall scrutinise his notes, and have a copy made available for you, Mr Maddox Brown. Any questions?"

The solicitor looked at Gus for the first time over the top of his half-moon spectacles.

"I'm happy to proceed," he said, "at this stage."

Gus touched the pen in his jacket pocket. He had no intention of using it to make notes, regardless of what they said. Annie Morgan had already started recording the interview. If Gus needed the transcript in the future, he only had to ask.

"We went over the events of the evening of Saturday, the eighth of March back in 2014 to our satisfaction," said Dai Williams. "I want to focus on what occurred in the afternoon."

"You know what happened," muttered Shaun Corbett.

"Yeah, we drove to the rugby club to get Kendall's dogs," said Vaughn.

"There was nobody around," said Shaun, "so we grabbed the pups, tied them up in the back of the van, and got out of Pontyclun as fast as we could. We were at the Bath turnoff when Kendall called."

"What did you do with Bubble and Squeak when you reached the site at Dilton Marsh?" asked Dai Williams.

"Who?" asked Shaun.

"Those were the names Alexa Kendall had given to the puppies. Surely, you must have heard her talking to them in the park?"

Both men shook their heads.

"You offered Ivan Kendall five hundred pounds for the dogs when you first called on him at the rugby club. Is that correct?"

"We wanted to know if he realised what was a fair price," said Shaun.

"Shut it, Shaun," said Vaughn.

"Perhaps the thousand pounds you demanded during that phone call on Saturday afternoon was also a test to learn whether Ivan Kendall knew how valuable they were?"

"It's not our fault if people don't know the value of things," said Vaughn. "We've got to make a living."

"On Saturday night, you had had two bites at the cherry," said Dai Williams. "You killed Ivan Kendall to get hold of the thousand pounds he'd brought with him, plus you still had the pups stored on the caravan site ready to sell to the highest bidder."

"This is old ground, Detective Inspector," said Maddox Brown. "What do you hope to achieve with this line of questioning?"

"I'm keen to learn what happened to the dogs," said Dai Williams. "Who did you sell Bubble and Squeak to, and when?"

"We never realised they had names," muttered Shaun. "Vaughn said we should tell the buyer they were called Storm and Thunder."

"We made ourselves scarce on Sunday morning before the town was awake," said Vaughn. "We drove back across the Severn Bridge with the dogs before the police had even moved to the railway station with their crime scene tape."

"Did you have a buyer lined up?" asked DS Morgan.

"We took photos of the dogs and posted them online," said Vaughn. "We used specialist sites where owners record the pedigrees of their dogs and the results of their matches. Of course, nobody posts their real identities, but one owner returned to us within hours."

"We recognised buildings and the distant hills in the photo's background showing his dog, Troy," said Shaun. "The village lies in the shadow of Pen y Fan in the Brecon Beacons. We're familiar with it as we spend months at the traveller's site in Cardiff."

"A pity you didn't know a potential buyer was so close," said Dai Williams. "You needn't have forced Ivan Kendall to travel to Westbury. He would still be alive today."

"Kendall was a fool," said Shaun. "Tell him, Vaughn, you understand it better than me."

"Kendall tried to con us they were pedigree puppies. We knew they were crossbreeds, and although they can be outstanding fighters, the bloodline is crucial in dogfighting circles. Those who display determination and perseverance are highly valued. Any that shies away from a fight gets dismissed as useless. If a dog has the right qualities, its offspring will display the same abilities. The guy who contacted us used Troy to breed several British fighting dogs."

"What were you asking for each of your pups?" asked Annie Morgan.

"Fifteen hundred for Storm. Two grand for Thunder," said Shaun. "We got it too."

Vaughn closed his eyes. His brother was a muppet.

"Why not make easy money when you can?" asked Shaun, ignoring his brother's body language. "Do you know how many hours grafting we needed to put in at houses in the valleys to get paid that much?"

"Where was the deal done?" asked Dai Williams.

"In a lay-by near Merthyr Tydfil," said Vaughn. "We handed over the dogs, and the buyer gave us the three-and-a-half grand in fifty-pound notes. That was the last we saw or heard of them."

"We're going to need the name," said Dai Williams.

Vaughn and Shaun shared a look. Gerwyn Maddox Brown leaned forward in his chair.

"Perhaps we could take a break there, Detective Inspector? My clients need a break."

"Shall we say fifteen minutes?" asked DS Morgan.

"That should be sufficient," smirked the smarmy solicitor.

"What do you think?" asked Dai William after the door closed behind the three men.

"Keep going as you are, Dai," said Gus. "no need to change tack just yet. I think the brief will convince them to cooperate further. It won't harm them, and it might benefit them."

"Ivor Lewis," said Vaughn Corbett when they returned to the interview room with their escort.

DS Annie Morgan left the room to get a colleague to

start the hunt for Ivor Lewis.

"You say you didn't hear what happened to the dogs after you left them with Ivor Lewis?" asked Dai Williams.

"We weren't interested," said Vaughn. "Don't look like that. We're no different to that Kendall bloke. He saw an opportunity to make easy money by selling the pups to someone who knew how to train them."

"But you killed him to ensure you took the profit he envisaged making, plus a tidy sum on top."

"Kendall wanted the dogs back," said Vaughn, "but he kept saying it wasn't right and we should get charged with theft. Kendall said he was going to the police when he got back home."

"If only he'd paid up and shut up, things wouldn't have turned out the way they did," said Shaun.

Gus shifted position in his chair. Gerwyn Maddox Brown looked in his direction, but Gus didn't speak.

"Sorry, lads," said Dai Williams as DS Annie Morgan returned to the room. "That doesn't wash. You carried weapons to the railway station for a reason. There's no point trying to deflect the blame for Kendall's death by saying he brought it on himself."

"We've given you Lewis's name; that should be worth something," said Vaughn.

"I'm sure we will take it into account, Vaughn," said Dai Williams. "We may have further questions after we've spoken to Ivor Lewis. Interview ended ten fifty-four."

DS Annie Morgan joined Gus and Dai Williams in the DCI's office.

"Lewis is a character we've come across before," she said. "He's a small-time villain who fences property stolen from farmers and smallholders in and around Pen y Fan. The RSPCA charged him with animal welfare offences last year. Not a pleasant person. He'll be here within the hour, guv."

"You had better let us speak with him alone, Gus," said Dai Williams, "we don't want to push it."

"I agree," said Gus. "I can walk into the centre, find a place to have lunch, and get back here at two o'clock."

"We've got a canteen here," said Annie Morgan.

"Gus is better off in the city centre," said Dai.

"Do you think you'll have something for me by two o'clock?" asked Gus.

"We can but try," said Dai.

Gus found a café within a fifteen-minute walk of the South Wales Police HQ.

As he scanned the menu for something that wouldn't repeat on him all afternoon, Gus remembered that slice of bara brith Kassie gave him. He'd slipped it into his desk drawer after returning to the office—and forgotten it.

Gus stuck to something nobody could screw up. He ordered a ham and cheese toastie and a black coffee. As he made his way back to the police station, rain fell from a cloudless sky.

Gus got through Reception in no time and was outside Dai Williams's office by a quarter to two. A peep through the window showed that Dai was still in the interview room.

Five minutes later, DS Annie Morgan came along the corridor.

"No joy, I'm afraid," she said. "At first, Ivor couldn't remember the Corbett brothers, but we reminded him that the RSPCA was only a phone call away. If he wanted to avoid a surprise inspection, he should start remembering. Lewis claimed it was a genuine transaction. The brothers named a price. He agreed and paid them in cash. When Dai asked about the dogs, he said they had a couple of fights each, performed well, and sold them at a profit after a year."

"That's promising," said Gus. "Did he give you a name for the buyer?"

"Buyers," said Annie. "we've got zero chance of tracing them. Ivor Lewis said he advertised on the Dark Web, secured the animals in cages to transport them by rail, then as soon as the money appeared in his bank account, he took the cages to Cardiff Central station. The arrangement was for the buyers to collect the dogs from the destination station. One dog went to Manchester, the other to Gravesend."

DI Dai Williams joined them in the corridor.

"I think that's as far as I can go," said Gus.

"It was always going to be a tough ask," said Dai Williams. "If those dogs survived this long, the training they've received from Lewis, and whoever's had them since, will mean that the dogs Alexa Kendall knew are long gone."

"My sister works out at West Point," said Annie, "at the Dogs Home. Why not drive over there? It will take you fifteen minutes. I'll tell Billie to expect you. By the sound of it, the Kendall girl was a good owner. They have plenty of animals longing for TLC."

"I'm getting sentimental in my old age," said Gus. "Perhaps I should just get in the car and drive home."

"You'll never forgive yourself," said Annie. "Do you have kids? Even when they're out of their teens, they still get a buzz from receiving a special gift from their parents. Alexa Kendall won't be any different. She doesn't have a father figure in her life, and it's only a few days since your guys got her and her mother back together. What you've got in mind could seal the deal in my book."

"You're wise beyond your years DS Morgan," said Gus.

"My late wife and I never wanted children, so I've never witnessed a child's reaction to a surprise present. I bow to your superior knowledge. Point me in the right direction to find your sister, and I'll let you two get on with nailing the lid on the Corbett brothers."

Gus left the South Wales Police HQ and soon found the industrial estate where the rescued dogs lived.

Billie Morgan was a carbon copy of her sister, Annie. She was two inches shorter, which might have denied her a career in the police. Billie let her mane of blonde hair fall where it pleased, while Annie's hair was short and neat.

"What breed of a dog were you interested in, Mr Freeman?" asked Billie.

"Not a clue," said Gus. "Nothing vicious, that's for sure."

"Where do you live? Town or country?"

"It wouldn't be for me," said Gus, "the couple I'm hoping to help live in Crickhowell."

"I've got a two-year-old Black Labrador that could do the trick. Come and see him."

Billie Morgan took Gus outside the main building, and Gus realised how many animals they had on the premises.

"The retriever is one of the nation's favourite breeds," said Billie, "they're active, friendly and loyal. I can run through the adoption process if you wish. We can arrange a home visit to vet the couple involved. Based on what Annie said, I don't think it will be an issue. Here he is. Meet Rex."

The black Labrador on the other side of the bars bounded from side to side. Gus couldn't remember the last time anyone was so pleased to see him.

"What happened to him?" he asked.

"Rex's owner died," said Billie, "She was in her eighties, lived alone, and had always had dogs in the family. Annie told me they believed the old lady had died in her sleep. A neighbour realised she hadn't seen her outside with Rex for two days and called the police. It's sad. Rex was lying at the foot of the stairs when they broke in. We nursed him back to health within seventy-two hours, and if you don't grab him, he won't be here for long. He's a lovely little fellow."

Gus couldn't tell one way or another. Rex was excitable and noisy. Gus accepted that millions of people found that endearing. He told Billie Morgan he would cover the adoption fee, and if Sally and Lexie Kendall didn't want to offer Rex a home, someone else would get a helping hand.

"Take a snap of Rex on your mobile phone," said Billie, "I presume you'll tell the family what you've done? See how the land lies, and then either come back to see me on the way back from Crickhowell or give us a ring."

Rex stood still long enough for Gus to capture several decent photos. Gus snapped Rex, leaping up at the bars and rolling around on the floor to add to the retriever's portfolio.

Billie and Gus walked back to the office. He paid the fee. It seemed ridiculously cheap compared to the sums that Bubble and Squeak commanded at around the same age. Billie handed him a card.

"Are you alright to find your way to Crickhowell?" she asked.

"I've got a satnav if I need it," said Gus.

"Have you got recovery, though?" asked Billie as she studied Gus's Ford Focus.

"There's nothing wrong with my car," he said, "apart from windows that stick."

"Good to meet you, Mr Freeman," said Billie, "I hope things work out. It's a good thing that you're doing."

"I'll call you as soon as the Kendalls have decided," said Gus.

An hour later, Gus parked the Focus outside the house where Sally Kendall lived under her new name, Sammy Prosser. He hoped Lexie was still with her mother.

Gus looked at his watch. Four o'clock. Sammy worked at an estate agency in town. It could be half-past five before she arrived home. He called Suzie at London Road to warn her he might not get home until eight o'clock. As he got out of the car, he noticed movement in the front room of the house. Somebody was home.

An attractive young woman answered the doorbell.

"Lexie Kendall?" asked Gus.

"Who's asking?"

"My colleagues brought you here last Saturday afternoon," said Gus. "Neil Davis and Luke Sherman work for me. My name is Freeman, Gus Freeman. Can I come in and talk to you for a few minutes?"

"You're a police officer too?"

"I was a Detective Inspector before I retired. They call me a consultant now. Here's my ID card. What time will Mum get home?"

"Not long now, she finishes at half-past four on a Wednesday."

Lexie walked to the lounge and pointed to the settee under the window.

Gus took a seat. Lexie sat in a chair to his left and tucked her legs under her bottom.

Gus took his mobile phone out of his pocket and laid it on the coffee table.

"Are you interviewing me?"

"Nothing like that," said Gus. "I'm sorry if I appear at sixes and sevens. This is unfamiliar territory for me. Look, my boss asked me to take another look at your father's case. We found his killers this time, and they will get locked up for a considerable period. Ever since I learned about Bubble and Squeak, I wanted to make up for the police not being able to find them for you in the days after your Dad died."

"I don't expect to see them again," said Lexie. "Dad was going to sell them, anyway. He warned me not to get too attached to them."

"But you did, didn't you?"

Lexie nodded.

Gus opened the phone and called up the images from the Dogs Home.

"He looks a little poppet. Is he yours?" asked Lexie.

"No, Rex is yours if you want him," said Gus. "I'm sure you'll be able to persuade your mother to give it a shot. If you think you can give Rex a home, I'll call the lady I met this afternoon, and she'll contact you to make the arrangements."

"I'm starting my studies soon," said Lexie. "I plan to set up a mobile hairdressing business. He could come with me in the car. We wouldn't leave him on his own. Mum can take him with her now and then. Her boss is a dog lover. It would be brilliant. Are you sure it's alright? Don't we need to pay anything?"

"That's been taken care of, Lexie," said Gus. "Courtesy of Wiltshire Police."

The look on the young girl's face was a picture. Gus remembered what Billie Morgan said: that kids never tired of receiving surprise presents from a parent. Was this how it felt to be a father?

"I can't wait for Mum to get home," said Lexie.

"I'll make that call then, shall I?"

"Yes, please, and thank you again."

Gus picked up his mobile phone and left the excited Lexie Kendall on the doorstep.

He walked to the car, drove out of Crickhowell, and parked in the nearest layby to call Billie Morgan.

"Did it give you a warm feeling, Mr Freeman?" she asked after he told her the good news.

"You might need to talk to your sister," he replied. "Ask her how it feels to solve a stubborn case. For me, this afternoon was as if I'd put a missing piece into a jigsaw. I could see the picture already, but it wouldn't be complete without it."

"Safe journey home, Mr Freeman," said Billie.

Chapter Six

GUS ARRIVED BACK at the bungalow just before seven. He parked his Focus next to the Golf and told it to sleep well.

Suzie was in the kitchen. "Was your journey to Crickhowell a success?" she asked.

"It was," said Gus. "Today proved to be a good day all around. I can draw a line under the Kendall case. We've done what we can."

"Back to reality in the morning," said Suzie.

"We can start interviews tomorrow," said Gus. "I haven't decided who will do what on this case yet. Neil might be best to take with me when I visit the murder site."

"We haven't discussed this new case yet," said Suzie. "Is it something I might remember?"

"Stacey Read?" asked Gus.

"Gablecross didn't get far with that one if I remember it right. Jack Sanders thought it was a sexual assault that escalated to something more. He believed there was a gang of lads from the nearby estate involved."

"Stacey had two knife wounds to her body and was half-undressed," said Gus.

"Could those wounds have killed her?" asked Suzie.

"They weren't superficial," said Gus. "but treated quickly, she had a chance. Although the autopsy found no evidence of sexual assault, bruises on the body suggested a sexual motivation behind her death. I can see why Jack Sanders followed the route he did, but how he leapt from a single attacker to a gang beats me."

"We don't know that part of Swindon as well as Jack did, Gus. Perhaps it was more likely that teenagers gathered in groups at night back then. Safety in numbers. With the increased activity on county lines, I don't believe you'd find many kids wandering close to that nature reserve alone."

"Your right, of course. Jack didn't find the lone teenager arguing with Stacey that night. Nor did he collect a list of names for the so-called gang members. The coroner had little evidence on which to decide. He decided Stacey drowned quickly after getting stabbed and deemed it an unlawful killing."

"Police appealed for people to come forward if they were in the nature reserve that night," said Suzie. "You know how well those appeals do. The silence was deafening."

"I'm not looking forward to interviewing the family members," said Gus. "Stacey was only thirteen with her entire life ahead of her. For different reasons, the three adult females will blame themselves to a degree. Her younger sister will still miss her. Stacey was a part-time carer for Lucy, too, based on the murder file report. Families, eh?"

"Do you mind if I ask a question, Gus?" asked Suzie.

"Anything," he replied.

"Did you ever want kids?"

"A difficult one to start with, I see. Tess was a teacher when we met," said Gus. "Before she moved to take a job at the college in Salisbury years later, she had taught for over twenty years. Kids surrounded Tess throughout her working life. Tess never expressed a desire to have children of her own. I didn't press her on the subject; perhaps I should have. You know me well enough to understand how I spend my time. I concentrated on work. The only thing I strived for in my career was the satisfaction of solving a crime and seeing the guilty party in prison. I wasn't interested in climbing the greasy pole like Geoff Mercer. The years slipped past, and then it wasn't an issue anymore. If it ever had been. We never discussed it and never argued over it. After Tess died, I spent days at the allotment, watching weeds grow. There were lots of questions for which I didn't have the answers. Yours was one of them. Did I ever want kids? I decided you don't miss what you never had. A lady I met this afternoon made me think about that question again. I saw Lexie Kendall's face when I showed her pictures of a black Labrador waiting for her and her mother to adopt. We never had pets at home when I was a kid. I couldn't understand why those owners I met on the Mark Malone case felt so passionate about their pups. As I considered the trauma Lexie had suffered since she was fourteen, it amazed me how the thought of having a dog to care for could transform her life."

"You're a big softie under that gruff exterior, Gus Freeman," said Suzie.

"I think I did the right thing today for a change," said Gus. "My stomach is telling me it's been too long since that toastie I had in Cardiff. Why don't I stick to my selfless kick and cook for you? It's been a while."

Suzie could tell the shutters had fallen again on her

partner's emotions. Gus wasn't the first copper she'd known who found the only way to deal with the dramas they dealt with was to pretend that nothing affected them. It didn't always end well.

"Right," she said, "but only if I can sit in the kitchen with you and watch a master at work."

"Mmm," said Gus, "I'm a big softie, and you're a frustrated stand-up comedian. Come on, then. Tomorrow I've got to delve into a thirteen-year-old girl's brief, tragic life. You don't get many laughs out of that experience."

Thursday, 19 July 2018

GUS HAD CONTINUED his good deeds for the day by cooking breakfast. He and Suzie left for work at the same time this morning. As he drove into Devizes following the Golf, he reflected on the evening they'd spent together.

The lamb steaks and vegetables had proved a success. It always pays to have a bottle of Merlot handy when serving lamb without an accompanying sauce.

This morning at breakfast, there had been a straightforward conversation between them. Similar to many other mornings since they became a couple. But nothing as deep as last night. Gus wondered what had sparked that. Should he have asked Suzie whether she wanted children in reply?

Suzie waved a hand as she turned into the London Road car park, and he flashed his lights in response. Gus continued driving towards the Old Police Station office, wondering why a thirty-three-year-old woman would throw her lot in with a sixty-two-year-old widower if she were desperate to start a family.

Gus hadn't gotten a satisfactory answer when he parked beneath the Crime Review Team office. The picture of Suzie on the steps of the building she had just left after the Eron Dushka case ended convinced him DI Ferris was a career copper intent on reaching the top. He had realised how much he wanted to be part of her life that day. Nothing had changed. It wouldn't surprise him if he lived with an Assistant Chief Constable a few years from now. As long as it wasn't Geoff Mercer, he could live with that.

"Good morning, guv."

Blessing Umeh had arrived.

"Hello, Blessing," said Gus. "Your reversing is improving. I can see the white lines on both sides of your car."

"Dave's helped me," said the Detective Constable as they travelled up in the lift together.

"You gave the young man another chance then," said Gus.

"We had lunch in Chippenham on Sunday," said Blessing. "Small steps, guv. My parents will want to meet him if they learn I'm spending too much time away from the Ferris farm."

"Ah, Maryam and Jackie talk regularly."

"My mother calls me on Wednesday evenings and expects a call from me at the weekend. But since they visited Worton, my mother also calls Mrs Ferris asking for recipes, advice on plants she saw in the garden, anything that allows her to check that I'm behaving myself."

"The joys of being a parent of an only child," said Gus.

"I love them dearly," said Blessing, "but they can be a trial."

The others were already at work when they entered the office.

"As everyone's here," said Gus. "I can update you on my

visit to Cardiff and Crickhowell yesterday. Vaughn and Shaun Corbett sold the dogs for three thousand five hundred pounds to a character called Ivor Lewis within days of the murder. Lewis trained the dogs, found opponents for them, and then sold them at a profit to two people through the Dark Web. There's little chance of tracking those transactions, and we must assume the dogs are beyond help. I adopted a black Labrador at the Dogs Home on the West Point Industrial Estate and then drove to Crickhowell, where I met Lexie, waiting for her mother to get home from work. One look at the photos of the dog was enough for her to say they would arrange to take Rex in and give him a wonderful home."

"Wow," said Lydia. "That was a result. What did her mother have to say?"

"I left before she got home," said Gus, "I'd done what I set out to do. No point in getting involved further. I'd spent enough time away from our remit as it was. Right, that's a solid, black line under the Kendall case. We've got a new case to pursue."

Luke looked at Neil to see his colleague raise one eyebrow. That was typical of Gus Freeman.

The crusty detective has a soft centre but doesn't want people to get used to seeing it.

"I've got a list of names, guv," said Luke. "Six interviews lined up for whoever you think should take them."

"Alex and Lydia, you can interview Vanessa Nicholls," said Gus. "Luke, you and Blessing can visit Mary Bennett."

"Do you want me to hold the fort here, guv?" asked Neil.

"We're off to Rushey Platt and then to Gablecross, Neil. After we've studied the murder site and its surroundings, we'll ask your mate, Jake, for the names of detectives that worked with Colonel Sanders on this case. I don't want to involve him if possible."

"What about Debbie Read and her daughter, guv?" asked Luke.

"I'll see them," said Gus. "I may need one girl with me. Lucy will be fourteen now and need a responsible adult present."

"Lucy's mother will want to be there, surely, guv," said Lydia.

"I don't think for one minute that Debbie Read killed Stacey," said Gus, "but Lucy may have secrets that the sisters kept from their mother. We'll get nothing from the young girl if her mother is listening. I'll talk with Debbie first and then explain why we want to talk to Lucy alone. We'll take the necessary action if she objects."

"Stacey's father, Pat Read, is on the list for tomorrow, guv," said Luke.

"That's five, Luke," said Gus. "Who was number six?"

"Christine Moseley, Head Teacher at Stacey's school. Ms Moseley has been in charge for eight years, so she knew Stacey from the day she arrived at the Academy from junior school. I thought she could offer an unbiased view of Stacey's behaviour in the weeks before her death. She could help with possible names for teenage lads that might associate with Stacey out of school."

"Fair enough, Luke," said Gus. "Ms Moseley's input will be something to compare with what Gablecross offers. Whether either angle will locate the mystery youth arguing with Stacey on the night she died, who knows?"

"When do we start?" asked Alex Hardy.

"Vanessa Nicholls starts work at two o'clock," said Luke. "I'll give you a number. Just call and tell her you're on your way."

"Is Mary Bennett retired?" asked Neil. Luke nodded.

"Blessing and I can get away as soon as I've given everyone the relevant contact details. Stacey's grandmother will be in throughout the day."

"Come on then, Neil," said Gus. "We'll drive over to the nature reserve. You can call Jake Latimer when we're ready to leave. We'll find someone else to help us if he's not in the office. I want to avoid Gareth Francis if possible. I met a PCSO called Travers when I stumbled upon the Gary Burnside murder. Travers had more common sense than most of the others at Gablecross. With luck, he'll be at a loose end."

Fifteen minutes later, the Old Police Station office was empty. The game was afoot.

"Did you find Gus's behaviour odd this morning?" Lydia asked Alex as he manoeuvred his car into town centre traffic from the car park.

"Odd, in what way?" he replied.

"He glossed over the details of the dog adoption, for one thing. It must have cost two or three hundred pounds. London Road wouldn't sanction that, so it came out of his pocket. Then, he didn't hang around to share the good news with Mrs Kendall. Gus got out as fast as he could."

"I spotted Luke and Neil sharing a look when he made those remarks," said Alex. "They started the ball rolling by reuniting Sally and Lexie. Gus thought it warranted a follow-up. I'm sure he cleared it with the ACC. It's a departure from the usual way we deal with completed cases, I admit."

"It's the female touch," said Lydia. "He's mellowed since Suzie Ferris moved in."

"I'm sure you're right," said Alex. "You haven't shared your good news with him yet, have you?"

"We don't want him suffering from emotional over-load," said Lydia.

"HAVE you ever been to this part of Swindon before?" Alex asked.

"No, only the main shopping centre and one of the retail parks on the outskirts."

"Penhill hasn't got a great reputation in the press, but it's only a minority that causes trouble. The streets where Vanessa Nicholls and Mary Bennett live are only a five-minute walk apart. They keep the community spirit I associate with the railway town that was dying when I was a kid. The new builds scattered around the borough are a mish-mash of design. No wonder they don't possess the same sense of belonging."

"No sign of Luke in the streets we've passed," said Lydia. "Are we nearly there?"

"Two more junctions to negotiate, and we'll be there," said Alex, "I was taking it slow. With any luck, Vanessa Nicholls will put the kettle on at ten o'clock."

Two minutes later, Lydia was knocking on the door of No46.

"Are you the police?"

The lady who answered the door wore a housecoat and flip-flops. Her dark hair was piled high on her head and wrapped in a towel.

"Vanessa Nicholls?" asked Alex.

"That's me,"

"I'm DS Hardy, my colleague Ms Logan Barre, and I want to talk to you about your niece's murder."

"Wiltshire Police wanted to take a fresh look at the

case," said Lydia. "They handed it to us. We work for a Crime Review Team. Can we come in?"

"Of course, sorry, I've only just got out of bed. Come through to the kitchen. I was going to make myself a brew. Tea or coffee?"

"Coffee, please," said Lydia. "White for him. Mine's black, both with one sugar."

"We understand from our colleague, DS Sherman, that you start work at two o'clock," said Alex.

"I work for Bromford, where I help provide specialist housing support," said Vanessa Nicholls. "I'm only part-time now, so I need to keep my other job."

"Something that involves late nights?" asked Lydia.

"I work behind the bar at a nightclub in Old Town."

"Was that your main occupation back in February 2015?" asked Alex.

"No, I've had several jobs since then. When Stacey went missing, I worked nine to five with the Nationwide Building Society. That was why the girls stayed over so often. I was always available in the evenings and at weekends."

"Your husband, Barry, had moved out by then?" asked Alex.

"He left me in 2008," said Vanessa. She removed the damp towel from her head and threw it on the kitchen floor next to the washing machine. "I didn't miss him that much; Barry spent most of the week driving abroad, anyway. Then, one Friday night, he didn't bother coming back."

"The girls started staying with you soon after, did they?" asked Lydia. "Your sister, Debbie, thought it would help, I suppose?"

Vanessa snorted.

"You are joking? Debbie off-loaded those girls onto Mum

as often as she could. Stacey stayed with Mum while Debbie was in the hospital having Lucy. Then, when she brought her home to Gorse Hill, it was six months before Debbie was ready to cope with two kids. Debbie started on me when it got too much for Mum to cope. Could I take them for a few hours? The girls enjoyed spending time with Auntie Vanessa. They said could they stay over. I should have called a halt, but if I had, I would have sent my mother to an early grave."

"Did Debbie find looking after the children difficult from the outset?" asked Lydia.

"You know Pat?" asked Vanessa.

"Her ex-husband, who works at the Honda factory?" said Alex. "Yes, we know about him."

"Debbie and Pat met on New Year's Eve 2000. She fell for Stacey in the spring. The wedding took place a month before the birth. In every photograph, my sister is holding a giant bouquet in front of the bump."

"Even if Pat thought they had forced him into the marriage, they still had a second child, Lucy," said Alex.

"Pat's an odd bloke," said Vanessa. "His job involves a lot of precision work, which typified his routine. He wanted his meals on the table at a specific time. Pat couldn't stand the disruption to his timetable that a couple of kids brought. Debbie got Mum to take one or both of the girls as often as possible, but in the end, Pat decided marriage wasn't for him. He left Debbie in 2007. I've got friends who live in Moredon. They tell me Pat works all week, washes the car on Saturday morning, shops at Waitrose on Saturday afternoon, and that's it. They rarely see him. He's got no social life."

"He wasn't interested in getting access to the girls?" asked Lydia.

"Not in the slightest. Pat turned his back on them as soon as he was out the door. Like I said, odd."

"What about Stacey?" asked Alex. "She was thirteen and street-smart, according to the evidence we've got. Wasn't she wondering about her Dad? Didn't she want to ask him why he'd left her when she was six?"

"Stacey asked me if it was her fault that her Dad left one time when they stayed. I told her not to be silly. It wasn't her fault. Her Mum and Dad couldn't make it work, like Uncle Barry and me."

"How did she react to that?" asked Lydia.

"She said, I knew it. Dad left because of Lucy."

"You had to put her right, I assume?" said Alex.

"I told her it was nobody's fault, but I'm not sure she believed me."

"Would you run through the events of that Sunday when Stacey first went missing?" asked Alex.

"I spent the day catching up with chores around the house and went shopping. Mum called at around six while I was washing my dinner things. She said the girls had gone home and reminded me Stacey was staying the night. I told her it was the first I'd heard. It made no odds to me. I wasn't going anywhere. So I waited, but Stacey didn't arrive. I thought Mum had got it wrong. Debbie didn't call either, so I forgot it."

"So, you were unprepared for her staying here?" asked Lydia.

"Look, I've got two bedrooms and that sofa bed. What's to prepare? If one of them arrived, we could make up the bed in a couple of minutes. When they were younger, they slept together. After Stacey started to grow, she wanted to be on her own. Lucy went in the second bedroom, Stacey slept in my bed, and I stayed downstairs."

"What happened on Monday morning?" asked Alex.

"I got up and went to work," said Vanessa.

"When did you realise that Stacey was missing?" asked Alex.

"Debbie called me on Tuesday evening. I hadn't long got in from work. But I needed some shopping, so I was later than usual."

"Were you surprised that Debbie waited until Tuesday evening?" asked Alex.

"Debbie must have assumed she was with Mum or me. Lucy wasn't much help. We could have started the search earlier if she said she hadn't seen her sister at school on Monday."

Stacey was already dead, thought Alex. You couldn't have saved her. But if they had found her body sooner, the evidence might not have got contaminated by canal water and the rats.

"Debbie didn't contact the police until she was on her way to work the next morning," said Alex. "A phone call on Tuesday night was best, surely?"

"That's Debbie for you," said Vanessa. "She was probably watching a programme on TV and didn't want to miss it."

"When did you go to your Mum's to check on Stacey?" asked Lydia.

"That was Tuesday night," said Vanessa. "I called Mum, but she never answered. Debbie asked me to see if Stacey was there. It was freezing out, but my sister stayed warm while I had to walk to Mum's. She had gone to bingo and didn't get home until ten."

"We've learned Stacey took time off school, particularly in the weeks before she died. Did she stay here?"

Vanessa blew out her cheeks.

"First I've heard. No, evenings and weekends were when the girls came here. Mum covered the rest as far as I'm aware."

"How long has Debbie worked out at Dorcan?"

"She didn't work after she got married. Until Pat walked out," said Vanessa. "Debbie started there at sixteen and stopped when she was six months gone with Stacey. They offered this morning shift at the start of 2008. It fitted in with the schooling, but it was more to suit Debbie. Everything revolves around her."

"In the original investigation, detectives thought someone, or something, altered Stacey's plans to spend the night here. Why didn't they learn that she wasn't supposed to be here, anyway?" asked Lydia.

"Debbie told me not to say too much," said Vanessa. "It made it sound like she didn't care for the girls as she should. You know what the social services are like with latchkey kids. Debbie was frightened they would take Lucy from her too."

"If Stacey wasn't due here, do you have any idea why she left home that night alone?" asked Alex.

"I've asked myself that question a thousand times," said Vanessa.

"Did Stacey have a boyfriend?" asked Lydia.

"Someone older, with a car?" asked Alex.

Vanessa shook her head and frowned.

"There was nobody like that," she said. "Stacey mentioned boys from school who were mates. She was thirteen, and they grow up faster than when I was that age, but Stacey wasn't seeing an older bloke as far as I know. There were no signs. She hardly wore make-up. She wore jeans and loose tops, a baggy jacket, not tight tops, and short skirts. Inside the house, I could see her body changing, but she never flaunted it, unlike others of her age."

"Do you remember any mates from school that Stacey mentioned," said Alex. "Lads, that could have been the one Debbie heard had been arguing with Stacey at the top of Redpost Drive?"

"I don't know which ones she mixed with at school lived out that way," said Vanessa.

"We can sort out the likely lads when we talk with Ms Moseley, the school head teacher," said Alex.

"Ryan Lock, Wayne Page, and Kane Hatton were names I often heard," said Vanessa.

"Did Debbie ever tell you the name of that lady walking her dog that night?" asked Alex.

"Did she even ask her who she was?" snorted Vanessa. "She was in such a state she would have forgotten it before she got home. You'll ask her when you talk to her, won't you?"

"Yes," said Alex, "but it always helps to get corroboration."

"We asked about boyfriends Stacey could have known," said Lydia. "What about you? Your husband, Barry, left ten years ago. Surely, you've met someone since then?"

"Who says I've been looking?" said Vanessa.

"Between 2008 and February 2015, when Stacey died, you had a steady job with the building society. When did you leave?"

"I left not long after Stacey's death, but I'd had my hours cut in 2010. That's when I started looking for part-time jobs to supplement my income."

"So, you looked for bar work at clubs similar to the one in Old Town?"

"I've worked in pubs since I was eighteen," said

Vanessa. "I could always pull a pint, chat to customers. I had a dozen landlords prepared to offer me work."

"You're still an attractive woman," said Lydia, "what are you now, late thirties?"

"Early forties is close enough," said Vanessa. "I'm three years older than my sister."

"So, take this nightclub, for instance," said Alex. "You get plenty of men in there, late at night. Quite a wide age range, some married, some single, and the owners encourage them to drink and lose their inhibitions. Plenty think they stand a chance with the young ones writhing on the podiums. Others know they're punching above their weight and decide they prefer the more mature woman. Did you ever take home one of those with a more discerning palate?"

"What if I did? I have needs, too," said Vanessa.

"Was Stacey ever here when someone stayed the night?"

"There was a bloke I saw for a month or two when I worked at a pub in Wichelstowe. He could still have been here one morning when the girls arrived to stay for the day. There was never a time when I left them alone to go to work. Nor did anyone turn up late at night when they were sleeping here. It must have been a Sunday. Stacey was twelve, maybe."

"What was his name?" asked Alex.

"Rod Maidment. He's not married. I don't think he ever has been. He works at Honda, in a different section to Pat Read. When I knew him, Rod was always complaining he was overweight. Rod used to play loads of sports when he was younger. When he stopped, he piled on the pounds."

"How old is he?" asked Lydia.

"A few years older than me. The last time I saw Rod, he

was thin as a rake. I fancied him more when he had something to grab hold of."

"Where did you see him? In the nightclub in Old Town?"

"No, Debbie puts flowers on the canal bank on Stacey's birthday, Christmas, the anniversary, you know. I saw him in the street as I went there on the bus."

"Does Rod Maidment have a car?" asked Alex.

"He drove a new Honda when I knew him," said Vanessa.

"How far is his house from the nature reserve?"

"Several miles. Rod didn't live in Wichelstowe. His house was on the other side of Wroughton."

"Does Lucy still come to stay with you?" asked Lydia.

"What do you think? My sister won't let her out of her sight. Debbie didn't blame Mum, or me, for what happened, but she won't take any chances with little Lucy."

"We might have more questions later, Mrs Nicholls," said Alex, "but we'll let you get on. Many thanks for your help this morning."

"I hope you find the devil that did it this time," said Vanessa. "Stacey would have been a real beauty now."

Alex and Lydia left Vanessa with the memories of her niece.

"That was informative," said Lydia.

"The murder file didn't suggest a tension between the sisters. I wonder how Luke and Blessing got on with Vanessa's mother?"

Alex drove them back to the Old Station office. They would catch up with the others when they returned to base.

Chapter Seven

ALEX AND LYDIA searched Penhill for Vanessa Nicholl's address while Neil parked near the Redpost Drive junction. He'd driven to Swindon on the motorway, left the M4 at Junction 16, and completed the journey on the A3102 Wootton Basset Road.

Gus and Neil stood on the opposite side of the road from where the eyewitness saw Stacey Read arguing with a teenage lad. The volume of traffic at ten in the morning was high.

"The only way we'd get the same view as that dog walker is if we came here in February at seven in the evening," said Gus. "If you ignore the traffic, it's unlikely she could swear in court who she saw. The street lights don't give a great spread, do they?"

"We might need to check to see whether the council has replaced the lighting since 2015, guv," said Neil. "I see what you mean, though. On an empty street at night, with a dim pool of light, the best you could do is say two kids stood over the road. Debbie Read was convinced, though, because the clothing matched what Stacey wore that night."

"I wish we had the eyewitness's name, Neil," said Gus. "I'd like to know precisely how Debbie phrased that question.

"I've got the stopwatch on my phone ready, guv," said Neil. "Let's walk at a steady pace to the nature reserve entrance."

"Is that the only entrance, Neil?" asked Gus.

"There are steps near a footbridge further up the canal, guv. The steps would be closer to where the 'Dragonfly' turns back to head for the landing stage on its pleasure trips."

"We're sticking to this route because it's the nearest to Redpost Drive, is that it?"

"We don't have any evidence that she went this way, guv," said Neil.

"Nor does it suggest in the murder file that Gablecross found evidence Stacey entered from another direction," said Gus.

"Well, we know where they found Stacey's clothing, guv."

"Fair enough. If Stacey's hoodie and top got discarded between the entrance ahead of us and where the body went into the water, it was logical to assume she accessed the nature reserve from here."

"Five minutes so far, guv," said Neil, checking his phone. "It's not a direct route from here. We turn left, double back on ourselves before turning right, and then move into the reserve."

The two detectives soon stood next to the Wilts & Berks canal.

"Eight minutes, guv. We can walk along this stretch now to the top of the reserve. I've got the locations of the clothing items on my phone. These apps are a bonus, aren't they?"

"I'm sure you're right, Neil," said Gus.

They walked along the footpath for one hundred yards.

"Over there, guv. That was where officers found Stacey's hooded jacket. It snagged on a bush after getting ripped from her body."

"Wouldn't that be difficult, Neil? If it was zipped up and Stacey wore a scarf and gloves."

"The jacket was unzipped when found, guv," said Neil, "look, here's a photograph."

"Why would Stacey unzip her jacket on such a cold night? Where did they find her gloves?"

"Stuffed in the jacket pockets, guv."

"What about the scarf?"

"Recovered from the water close to the bush where she lost the jacket."

"Remind me what Stacey wore underneath. We assume she's running for her life now, yes?"

"Yes, guv. Debbie told the police Stacey wore a sweatshirt. They found that half in, half out of the water here. Just after that minor depression in the grass."

"Stacey probably stumbled there, said Gus, "because of the uneven ground. It would be easy to turn an ankle in the dark or pitch forward onto her knees. Did they find bruises on her legs?"

"Nothing recorded, guv," said Neil. "Her jeans could have got muddy, but after a week in the canal, there wouldn't be much to analyse."

"If she fell, it might explain how her attacker removed the sweatshirt," said Gus. "No zip or buttons; he just grabbed the bottom of the sweatshirt and dragged it over her head. Stacey got back on her feet, wrestled her way clear, and ran in this direction. How much further?"

"Eighty-five metres, guv," said Neil.

Gus and Neil stopped walking and stared into the stretch of the canal. On a warm summer's day like today, an idyllic spot.

"What's that over there near the water's edge, Neil?" asked Gus.

"It looks to be an Easter cross, guv. I expect Debbie or her mother put it here on April the first, Easter Sunday this year. No doubt there will be flowers for her at other times."

Gus sighed.

"I've seen the where for all the help it's been. Now I need to find the why."

"Let's walk back to the car, guv. I'll call Jake Latimer, and then I'll drive us out to Gablecross."

Forty minutes later, they headed for the detective squad room. Reception seemed to doubt that Jake Latimer was in the building. Gus said that Neil had just spoken to him.

"The desk sergeant still wasn't convinced, was he," said Gus.

Neil spotted his friend on the far side of the room by the window.

"You've hung onto the best seat in the room then, Jake," he said.

"Neil, how are you doing? Gus Freeman too. Morning, guv. Good to see you again."

"What can you tell us about the Stacey Read case?" asked Gus.

"The Colonel took charge," said Jake. "DI Raj Sengupta was his second-in-command. Although I worked on most cases with Theo Hickerton, I got assigned to that murder for a while."

"Come on, Jake, spill the beans," said Gus. "We don't have long."

Jake leaned back in his chair.

"Look, it was a mess from the start. First, the mother got involved, investigating alone, stirring up the media, and complaining we didn't take her daughter's disappearance seriously. Jack Sanders was still smarting from the lack of progress on the Burnside shooting. They should have given him a golden handshake and wheeled him into retirement. His heart wasn't in it."

"What was this Sengupta bloke like?" asked Gus.

"Green as grass, a brain the size of a planet, but useless with the public," said Jake.

"Where is he now?" asked Gus.

"With the Metropolitan Police, running a cybercrime team. Best place for him. In a dark room with a dozen screens."

"Was there any reason Debbie Read believed you dragged your heels?" asked Neil.

"There were no flags against the family," said Jake, "but when the desk sergeant took the details on Wednesday morning, Debbie kept stressing she hadn't known Stacey was missing. The sergeant asked why nobody called on Sunday night when Stacey didn't reach her aunt's house. As soon as he heard about the variety of places where the girl might have stayed, he decided she wasn't in danger. The mother had mislaid her, like forgetting which level she parked her car in the multi-storey. He tried to get Debbie Read to calm down and provide more details. Instead, she rabbited on about her husband and brother-in-law having walked out and that her Dad died last year. You know how it goes, Neil. Some days you ask yourself, why do the nutters always descend on the station when I'm working?"

"Surely, things improved once the body turned up?" asked Gus.

"Sanders and Sengupta picked up the case with immediate effect. I got assigned to it after a week. By then, we learned of the sighting out at Redpost, but Debbie Read isn't even a PCSO, and they can sometimes be next to useless. Mrs Read spoke to a lady walking her dog who said she saw Stacey arguing with another teenager. The timing and description were vague, yet when we heard Debbie Read's account on local radio, it had become solid gold. Stacey *was* there. We couldn't verify that because Debbie didn't record the woman's name, address, or contact number. According to Debbie, if you've read the murder file, the woman had kids who attended the same school as Stacey. She recognised her. Debbie denies asking the woman if she wore a grey hoodie, blue jeans, and a pink scarf and gloves. Or whatever it was. Raj Sengupta believed that Debbie described everything her daughter was wearing when she left home, and not surprisingly, her eyewitness didn't want to upset her by saying she had seen no one. Debbie was distraught on Wednesday night when she started that search for Stacey. She was on medication by the weekend. Jack thought her unreliable."

"Did uniforms do a house-to-house near Redpost Drive, trying to find the witness?" asked Gus. "What about the teenage boy? Were there any sightings of him, with or without Stacey, anywhere in Gorse Hill, Penhill, or near Rushey Platt? If a young lad killed Stacey, he would have been running away from the scene. No way could he calmly walk away."

"They tried to find the dog walker, but I don't need to

tell you how many there are in a place as big as Swindon. In the three weeks I worked on the case, we tried a reconstruction, which resulted in several hundred calls. No surprise. Every night of the week, residents around Swindon see young lads running through the streets. It happens after a football match. It happens when lads with knives are chasing members of another gang. On the other hand, it could just be a kid trying to get home before ten o'clock to avoid getting grounded. We got nowhere."

"Jack Sanders thought Stacey went to Rushey Platt willingly, and things escalated," said Neil.

"Jack had a bee in his bonnet about gangs," said Jake. "There were gangs around, but not on today's scale. We found no one from our usual suspects who we could place in the nature reserve vicinity. One thing common in our responses was that gang members swore blind they hadn't heard of Stacey Read. She didn't hang around with gangs. Okay, she was an attractive girl. It wouldn't be the first time three or four hooligans chased a girl and carried out a sexual assault. But nothing we learned placed anyone with the slightest potential for that type of assault in the nature reserve on the night in question."

"Something doesn't stack up," said Gus. "The murder file said that Stacey was street-smart. The person you're describing is an innocent, a Miss Goody Two Shoes. Once I read where and when the murder occurred, I wondered what possessed Stacey to go there - whether alone, with a boy, or with a gang. A street-smart girl would understand the dangers and avoid situations where she could get into trouble."

"Her reaction to the first attack was strange too, guv," agreed Neil. "If she accessed the nature reserve where we did, then if someone tried to assault her, why keep going in the opposite direction? Her escape route was one hundred yards behind her, back out onto Redpost Drive, with the possibility of getting help."

"Anything else you wanted to know?" asked Jake.

"You said we had no flags against the family, Jake," said Gus. "Did that include Pat Read?"

"Pat Read has no criminal record," said Jake. "Raj interviewed him as a matter of course. The father is always a potential suspect. Read decided marriage wasn't for him seven years before the murder. He walked away and rented property near the Honda factory. Everything checked out. Pat Read's never taken a day off work. His employers say his conduct is exemplary. Neighbours told us he keeps himself to himself. If it comes to that, they've never seen him with another woman or man. When asked whether he'd been in touch with his daughters since he left the family home, Read looked at Raj as if he was stupid. Why would I, he asked?"

"I can't wait to meet him," said Gus, "he seems an odd character. I know they exist, but I wonder what the teenage Debbie Bennett saw in Pat Read when they met?"

"Have you spoken to Debbie yet?" Jake asked.

"Not yet," said Gus, "we have people talking to Vanessa Nicholls and Mary Bennett this morning. When we return to the office, we may need to reconsider the next names on our list. I plan to see Debbie and Lucy separately tomorrow. If nothing else, Pat Read could climb the schedule for his curiosity value."

"I wish you luck, whichever way you choose, guv," said Jake. "Those three women who so-called cared for Stacey were a slippery bunch. It was hard to know which one was telling the truth."

"We have more to learn, Jake," said Gus. "Thanks for

your input. Is that young PCSO Travers around these days?"

"Gareth Francis thought you spotted potential in the lad, so Travers is at college three days a week. He's on a sandwich course or something. I don't know the details, but they never offered me that support when I started."

"Is that the same Gareth Francis you thought was a muppet, guv?" laughed Neil.

"The very same, Neil, but Gareth's realised it pays to listen to the voice of experience. Does Travers have a first name, Jake? I've heard no one use it."

"He hates it, guv," said Jake. "So, he asked that we treat him like one of those pop stars that goes by a single name, like Prince. HR went along with it, and it's his human right or something. The world's changing, guv, isn't it?"

"It left me behind a while back, Jake. Come on, Neil, let's get back to the office."

MARY BENNETT WATCHED the car pull outside her door and manoeuvre into the remaining parking space. He was good, whoever he was. The tall, handsome driver stood on the pavement as a solid-looking black woman emerged from the passenger side. The woman checked Mary's door number against a folder she held, and the couple walked up the path.

These must be the coppers she was expecting. Mary levered herself from her chair and pushed her Zimmer frame into the hallway and the front door.

Luke heard the chain slide back and the door unlocked.

"Are you the police?" asked Mary Bennett.

Luke and Blessing produced their warrant cards and showed them to Mary for inspection.

"You had better come in," said Mary, reversing her walking frame and turning back into the front room. Mary edged across the room and sat back down.

Luke moved a dining chair and sat beside Mary. He'd spotted her hearing aid. Blessing seated herself under the window and studied the room. Apart from the hallway, there were just two rooms on the ground floor: this room and the kitchen. There must be two bedrooms and a bathroom upstairs.

"I'm DS Luke Sherman," said Luke, "my colleague is DC Blessing Umeh."

"Blessing?" said Mary Bennett. "I don't think I've heard that name."

"I was the only girl in the playground at school with that name," said Blessing.

"Do you know why we've come here today, Mary," asked Luke.

"I haven't lost my marbles, young man," said Mary. "You want to ask about Stacey."

"It must have been awful," said Luke, "when Stacey went missing. Then to discover she was dead was a tragic loss. Only thirteen years old."

"I didn't know she was missing, did I? Not at first. Debbie didn't let me know. Vanessa stood on my doorstep when I got home from bingo Tuesday night. That's when I found out."

"How did you feel looking after Stacey and Lucy so often?" asked Luke.

"Debbie had a dreadful time with Stacey. The pregnancy wasn't without problems, and Stacey was a breech delivery. It was one thing after another, and Pat was useless. I started going to Gorse Hill to help when Pat was at work.

When Debbie fell for Lucy, I offered to look after her and Stacey."

"Wasn't the second pregnancy any easier?" asked Blessing.

"It should have been, but Debbie kept moaning and groaning that it was too much. Harry warned me. He said I was letting myself in for hard work after Lucy arrived, but I couldn't turn my back on my daughter, could I?"

"Harry, was your husband, wasn't he?" asked Luke.

Mary pointed to a wedding photograph on the mantlepiece.

"Twelve years ago, he died," she said. "Lung cancer. He got diagnosed a week after Lucy's second birthday."

"Caring for Harry must have restricted the help you could offer Debbie," said Luke.

"Don't you believe it," said Mary. "My daughter told me she had her own life to lead. I spent as much time in Gorse Hill as I did here and at the hospital."

"At that stage, did the girls stay overnight with you?" asked Luke.

"Not until after Harry died," said Mary. "Debbie thought it helped me to have them here. She said she didn't want me to get lonely. I couldn't say no. I loved both of those girls. Vanessa won't give me grandchildren, so now it's only Lucy left. Debbie won't let her stay here."

"Debbie's more protective of her only surviving child," said Luke. "I suppose you can understand that."

"It's a pity she didn't think that way from the start," said Mary.

"What did you mean, Mary," asked Blessing Umeh. "When you said that Debbie had her own life to lead?"

"Where do you think she was when those girls came here?" asked Mary.

"We haven't spoken to anyone else but you so far, Mary," said Luke. "In the original investigation, detectives learned that you and Vanessa let the girls stay over now and then. I don't recall reading why Debbie couldn't look after them on those occasions."

"Debbie was out enjoying herself. She went to bingo in Greenbridge and met up with people from Dorcan, where she worked. They spent the rest of the night in a club some-where. What time she rolled home, I wouldn't know. The girls weren't allowed home until mid-afternoon on Sunday; I know that. My daughter needed to get over her hangover or get rid of any bloke she took home."

"This started after Harry died and Pat had left, I take it," said Luke.

Mary nodded.

"Harry was sixty-nine," said Mary, "which is quite an age when you smoke forty a day for fifty years. Pat left within a year of Harry's passing. That's when I started having the girls here more often. Twice a week, on average."

"The girls stayed on school nights too, did they?" asked Blessing.

"They have bingo somewhere every night of the week, love," said Mary. "Vanessa was working full time, Monday to Friday, so I covered a weeknight; Vanessa had them on the weekend."

"Were there many men Debbie took home after a night out?" asked Luke.

"Nobody's business but her own," said Mary. "Both of my girls are still attractive women who fell for blokes that walked out on them. Harry and I never interfered. It was their choice, and they had to make the best of it as they could. If they both looked for comfort now and then, what business is it of the law?"

"Provided nothing happened to the girls, then the law never gets involved," said Blessing. "Why was there confusion over who Stacey was staying with that Sunday night?"

"I was sure Debbie told me that our Vanessa had agreed to let Stacey stay," said Mary. "Debbie was such a scatter-brain; she could have made a mistake. Perhaps Debbie thought she'd called Vanessa to fix it, but it slipped her mind. So I packed Stacey and Lucy off home that Sunday evening and watched TV until nine o'clock. Then I went to bed. It was too cold to sit here any longer."

"Stacey staying at Vanessa's alone was a departure from the usual arrangements, wasn't it?" said Blessing.

"The girls always came here together for years," said Mary. "They slept in what used to be their mother's bedroom. Our two had separate single beds, but Harry put bunk beds in for Stacey and Lucy. Stacey slept on top, Lucy on the bottom. When Stacey started to develop, she felt self-conscious. Debbie agreed to let her stay at Vanessa's alone."

"When the girls stayed here, what did they do?" asked Blessing.

"They watched TV. I showed them how to knit and crochet, baked cakes, and played board games. We did the things kids of their age do with their grandmother."

"I imagine that was changing too as Stacey grew older?" asked Blessing.

"Stacey received phone calls after she got her mobile phone on her thirteenth birthday," said Mary. "The calls were from her girlfriends from school."

"Did she get calls from boys, too?" asked Blessing.

"Have you seen a photograph of Stacey?" asked Mary.

Blessing had seen the crime scene photos. As she scanned pictures on the Welsh dresser on her left, she could see one of Stacey and Lucy sitting side by side in their school uniforms, taken not long before the murder.

"She was beautiful," said Blessing, "Lucy too."

"I notice a photo on the dresser with Stacey and Lucy at the seaside. Could she swim?"

"Like a fish," said Mary. "they both could. Debbie taught them."

"Did Stacey mention any boy in particular?" asked Luke.

"She never told me who rang her, but when Stacey and her friends chatted, a few names cropped up more than once. Ryan and Wayne must have been popular lads with the girls."

Luke made a note of the names.

"Did the girls ever ask after their father?" asked Blessing.

"For a while, after he left, Stacey would ask if it was something she did wrong. It was tough to explain to the poor child. She was only six. Both girls stopped asking where he'd gone after a year, and I never raised the subject. For a while, I think Lucy thought he'd died and gone to heaven, the same as Grampy. The events were so close together; Debbie seemed happy to let her roll them into one. Stacey was more aware of what had happened by the time she was thirteen."

"Did she ever say she wanted to contact him?" asked Luke.

"Never," said Mary.

"You can see lots of this street from that picture window, can't you?" asked Luke.

He'd spotted Mary watching their every move outside.

"I don't get out as much as I used to. My legs are in a

terrible state. There's not much on TV to interest me, especially in the summer."

"Were any cars outside when Stacey and Lucy left here?"

"The street's filled with them," said Mary. "It's difficult to find a parking space."

"I wondered whether an older boy with a car might have approached Stacey and arranged to meet her somewhere. The detectives back in 2015 weren't sure why she went from Gorse Hill to Redpost Drive or how she got there. Stacey might have caught a bus, but the police struggled to find a reason for the journey. Did Stacey know a boy, or someone older, from that part of town?"

"She could have known someone from school, I suppose," said Mary. "They come from right across Swindon at the Academy. I don't know about someone older. How would she meet them?"

"We understood that Stacey played truant from school in the weeks before she went missing," said Luke. "Also, she wanted to spend less time with her little sister and more time mixing with her friends on the nearby estate."

"You can't watch them twenty-four hours a day, can you?" said Mary.

"Would you say that Stacey was a sensible girl," said Blessing, "who knew right from wrong?"

"Debbie wasn't the best role model for a daughter, although it pains me to admit it," said Mary. "Vanessa and I did our best to keep Stacey on the right road. She knew better than to have a crafty fag behind the bike shed. I reminded her of what killed her Grampy. She saw the effect drinking had on her mother when she was still hanging out of her backside at six in the evening on a Sunday. Stacey would never smoke or drink. That only left two problems:

drugs and boys. Both of which are everywhere. I warned her the best I could about drugs, although I never had to cope with the volume and variety they have today. I can't swear she stayed away from them, but she showed none of the signs I read up on. Stacey seemed a sensible kid whenever she was around me, with her entire life ahead of her. It was a man or boy that stole that future from her, but whether he was someone Stacey knew or a stranger, I don't know."

"We've taken up enough of your morning, Mary," said Luke. "If we have further questions, may we come back?"

"Yes, dear," said Mary. "It's good to have someone here for a chat. Can you see yourselves out?"

"Is there anything I can get you before we leave, Mrs Bennett?" said Blessing. "I can make you a cup of tea and bring it through if you wish."

"A cup of tea would be lovely," said Mary. "You are a treasure. I've got Hobnobs in a tin by the kettle. Put one on the saucer for me if you would. Grab one for you both to eat in the car."

Luke watched Blessing disappear to the kitchen.

"Can I use your bathroom, please, Mary?"

"Of course," she replied. "Don't forget to put the toilet seat back where you found it."

Luke heard the whistle of the kettle as he went upstairs. He closed the bathroom door and stuck his head around the door to the smaller of the two bedrooms.

The bunk beds were still there. The bedclothes were what Luke imagined appealed to young girls. A layer of dust on the bedside cabinet suggested this room was more of a shrine these days. Luke slid open the drawers in the cabinet to see whether anything remained.

A diary would have been a bonus, but someone had

emptied the drawers. Luke left the bedroom and entered the bathroom to flush the toilet. As he trotted downstairs, Blessing emerged from the front room.

"Ready to go, Luke?" she asked.

He nodded.

"Thank you, Mary," he called. "Goodbye."

"Bye, love. Come again, won't you?"

"Do you enjoy a Hobnob, Luke?" asked Blessing when they returned to the car.

"I do, but they're better with a cup of coffee."

"I'll make you a cup when we get back to the office," said Blessing.

"I wonder what the others have found out," said Luke. "Mary's tale doesn't gel with what we thought we knew of Stacey, does it?"

"No," said Blessing, "and Debbie Read had more going on in her life than we thought."

ALL THREE CARS arrived back at the Old Police Station office within fifteen minutes of one another. Luke and Blessing enjoyed coffee and a biscuit when Alex and Lydia exited the lift. The four colleagues were comparing notes when Gus and Neil entered the office.

"That's three sessions finished and at least half a dozen to go," said Gus. "Neil, make us a coffee, please. If possible, we need to debrief this morning's interviews and then set up meetings for this afternoon."

After Gus and Neil had their coffees on the desk in front of them, the team dived in.

Gus listened to Alex and Luke as they relayed the high-lights of their meetings.

"So," said Gus after they'd finished. "According to

Vanessa, her sister offloaded the two girls as often as possible from a young age. Initially, Mary Bennett bore the brunt, but Vanessa got dragged into the parenting, mostly at weekends. Stacey believed it was her fault that her father had walked out. Both women heard her say that, and both assured her it wasn't her fault. It was just one of those things. Debbie asked Vanessa to lie when speaking to the police in the original investigation. Debbie didn't want the police to learn how often the girls weren't sleeping at home. Vanessa didn't know that Stacey was staying with her that Sunday night. Mary was confused about the matter. That may be significant. Did Stacey set up a meeting with someone and hope her mother wouldn't call Mary or Vanessa to double-check the arrangements?"

"Mary didn't know of any boyfriends Stacey could have planned to meet," said Blessing.

"Mary also knew Debbie took a fair number of lovers after her husband left her, but Vanessa mentioned nothing about that," said Alex.

"Vanessa gave you three names to confirm with the headteacher," said Luke. "One of them could be the boyfriend or the killer. Maybe, they were the gang of lads Jack Sanders suspected got involved, and they acted together."

"Jake Latimer said they couldn't link anyone with the Rushey Platt attack, " Lydia said. "If one of the three names Vanessa Nicholls gave you was a likely candidate for a sexual assault, it would have cropped up, surely?"

"What of this chap, Rod Maidment, guv?" asked Neil.

"We'll speak to him, Neil," said Gus. "Unless Vanessa was lying, there were only one or two occasions when the guy was still at her place after he slept with her. Maidment might not remember the girls and vice versa."

"The original investigation got off to a poor start, didn't it, guv?" said Blessing. "The desk sergeant didn't take the missing person's report seriously, and the shambles that followed stemmed from his half-hearted response."

"We can't change the past, Blessing. There are two things I need to learn from the interviews we've got ahead of us. First, why did the murder file state that Stacey Read was street-smart when everything we've heard suggests the opposite? Why did she run in the direction she did when her nearest escape route was directly behind her?"

"Blessing came up with another question, guv," said Neil. "I remembered it this morning as we walked beside the canal. If the stab wounds weren't fatal, why didn't Stacey attempt to get out of the water?"

"Did anyone check whether Stacey could swim?" asked Gus.

"I asked Mary Bennett, guv," said Blessing. "Debbie taught both girls to swim, and they were powerful swimmers."

"I wondered why you asked that, Blessing," said Luke. "I quickly searched the girls' bedroom to see whether Stacey had a diary, guv. But, unfortunately, there wasn't one there."

"I doubt she would have left it lying around for someone to read," said Lydia. "I know I wouldn't. If a diary existed, her Gran has thrown it away by now."

"Neil," said Gus, "can you call Debbie Read and arrange for us to meet her at Gablecross later this afternoon or at ten in the morning? Lucy should be at home; schools broke up for the holidays last week."

"Yes, guv," said Neil. "Who did you have in mind for the responsible adult when we speak to Lucy?"

"Try to get hold of Christine Moseley," said Gus. "If she hasn't flown away on holiday already, we could kill two birds with one stone. Debbie Read could hardly object to Ms Moseley taking her place."

"A bit late to complain now, guv," said Lydia. "Both her daughters spent more time with someone else than they did with their mother."

Neil made the calls. Christine Moseley wasn't available until the morning. Debbie needed to bring Lucy with her as her mother was too tired, so Luke scheduled the meetings for Friday.

Chapter Eight

Friday, 20 July 2018

SUZIE LEFT the bungalow at eight o'clock and drove to
London Road. They didn't have any deep and meaningful
conversations last night. Instead, Gus had arrived in Urchfont with his head filled with questions from the interviews
he and the Crime Review Team had conducted earlier in
the day.

Gus wanted to spend an hour on the allotment trying to
make sense of it all. Suzie elected to stay home to cook a
meal ready for when he reached home. When they got to
bed at around eleven, Suzie was no nearer deciding when to
broach the subject that had occupied her mind since last
weekend.

As he lay beside her, Gus recognised that the three
conversations at Gablecross Police Station in the morning
had to prove significant if they were ever to solve this three-
year-old mystery.

Gus spotted Neil's car as soon as the bonnet poked its head into the gateway. Gus opted to carry his jacket over his shoulder since the sun was already high in the sky. It could be a scorcher.

Neil had hardly completed his three-point-turn in the driveway when Gus opened the passenger door and sat inside.

"Blimey, Neil," he said. "It's baking in here. Don't tell me your windows don't work properly either."

"I've got air-conditioning, guv," said Neil, "but it's on the blink. So in anticipation of good news next week, I'm cutting back on unnecessary expenses."

"Were you expecting a pay rise, Neil?" asked Gus, and then the penny dropped.

"Melody might be expecting, is that it? That would be fantastic news, Neil."

"Thanks, guv. Please don't mention it to the others yet. Melody wants the doctor to confirm it after what happened last time. Let's say we're cautiously optimistic. Then we must get them over the finishing line."

"The doctors will know how best to avoid or ease the problems Melody suffered during the first pregnancy, Neil. I'm sure you'll follow their advice. Don't worry, I won't breathe a word, even to Suzie."

Gus and Neil signed in at Reception at Gablecross and followed the complicated signage to reach DI Francis's office.

"Just one hurdle to get over before we can get cracking at ten o'clock," said Gus.

He tapped on the office door, and Gareth Francis waved them inside.

"Good morning," said Gareth. "Interview Room 3 is at

the end of this corridor, the first room on the left. Jake Ingram tells me you're taking a second look at the Stacey Read case."

"We prefer to think of it as a fresh look, Gareth," said Gus. "We're speaking with Stacey's mother, her younger sister, and the girls' head teacher."

"Do you mind if I watch from the viewing room next door?" asked Gareth Francis.

"Good to see you're still willing to learn, Gareth," said Gus. "Oh, well done for giving PCSO Travers the opportunity for advancement. A wise move, even if it means you could salute him one day."

Gareth smiled. That unnerved Gus. The Welsh DI wasn't famed for his sense of humour. But, since moving from Devizes, something else positive had rubbed off on him here in Shrivenham.

"Very droll, Gus. I thought it wise to offer support if the mother protested your decision to exclude her from Lucy's interview. I could suggest I sit with her at the back of the room. The presence of a senior officer should reassure her that everything was by the book."

"What a generous offer, Gareth," said Gus. "I'll bear it in mind."

"You had better get along the corridor," said Gareth. "The desk sergeant will bring Mrs Read through any minute. If Ms Moseley gets delayed, I asked him if he could keep Lucy Read amused."

Gus and Neil left the office. Gareth Francis shuffled several papers, grabbed a notebook and pen, and followed them to Interview Room 3. As he entered the viewing room, he saw the door open, and a uniformed officer ushered in Debbie Read.

"Good morning, Mrs Read," said Gus. "Thank you for

attending this informal conversation this morning. As our colleague DS Sherman told you, we're re-visiting your daughter Stacey's death."

"Call me Debbie. It seems pointless to keep his name, but it's too much hassle to get it changed."

"As you wish, Debbie," said Gus. "I'm a consultant with Wiltshire Police. My name is Freeman. DS Davis is with me this morning. Can we start by running through the events leading up to February 2015? We'll try not to upset you unduly, but I'm sure you want to help us find out who was responsible for Stacey's death."

"Of course I do," said Debbie. "I take most of the blame. I should have been a better mother."

Neil studied the woman across the desk. She looked older than her thirty-eight years. Tragedy takes its toll in cruel and different ways.

Neil could see why men found Debbie attractive despite the dark roots visible among her blonde curls and a blouse and skirt that had suffered too many machine-wash cycles. Luke mentioned something similar yesterday afternoon when they discussed Vanessa Nicholls's testimony.

"She did nothing for me, Neil," he said. "Most of the officers at London Road would likely be on her like a rat up a drainpipe."

"Did you even want children?" asked Gus, bringing Neil's attention back on track.

"Of course I did," said Debbie, sitting straighter in her chair. "What sort of question is that?"

"I was wondering about you and Pat Read. Were you both keen to have a family?"

"We had little choice, did we? I was pregnant with Stacey within three months of meeting Pat. My Dad was a stickler for the bloke doing the honourable thing. Pat went along with it, although it seems he always blamed me. Pat said he felt trapped when we rowed in the months before he walked out."

"Did he have a case?" asked Gus.

"We always used a rubber," said Debbie, "so we were just unlucky."

"We've heard you had a tough time with Stacey," said Neil.

"I don't know who told you that. Stacey was good as gold."

"DS Davis meant during the pregnancy and immediately after," said Gus.

No, I didn't, thought Neil. It was a deliberate ploy. You suggested it in the car as we drove through Wroughton.

Debbie drew in her breath and let out a deep sigh.

"Some women sail through the nine months and pop their babies out like shelling peas. I was unlucky. I had a dreadful time of it for months, and then Stacey was a breech baby."

"You were glad of the support that your mother could provide," said Neil.

"We were a family. I would have done the same for Stacey if she'd lived. I'll be there for Lucy when the time comes. Which I hope won't be for several years yet."

"Did your husband lend a hand?"

"Never," said Debbie. "He was always at work. They didn't let fathers have paid paternity leave until after Lucy was born. Not that Pat would have taken time off if they had."

"That must have put a strain on the marriage," said Gus.

"I was too tired to get into an argument," said Debbie.

"We battled through the next two years, and then I fell pregnant with Lucy,"

"You and Pat continued to have normal relations," said Gus.

Debbie and Neil stared at him.

In the viewing room, Gareth Francis clicked his pen. That was worth making a note of.

"Pat wanted sex every other day," said Debbie. "I don't know if you consider that normal. He wasn't into kinky stuff if that's what you're wondering. Some days we didn't speak to one another, but for forty minutes every other night, it took me out of myself."

"Forty minutes?" asked Neil.

"Have you met him?" Debbie asked. "The clock governs Pat's entire world. His job at Honda started his fixation; it affected everything he did. As a result, he grew less interested in me and never bonded with the girls because they didn't fit into his time-sensitive regime."

"Did Pat have any hobbies? Did he spend time away from home, apart from for his work?"

"Not really. Pat's only passion was Honda cars. He has a brand new one every year, and that's where he lavished his attention. He still does, so people tell me."

"Your sister said he was an odd character," said Gus.

"Odd?" asked Debbie. "Do you know anyone who carpets their garage?"

Gareth Francis clicked his pen. What was wrong with putting down the old carpet? So he could wipe his feet and go straight into the utility room without trailing mud through the house.

"After Pat walked out, what happened then?" asked Gus.

"I needed Vanessa to take some of the load," said

Debbie. "Mum did her best, but after Dad died, she needed time to grieve. Well, each of us did, but if the three of us spent time with the girls, I thought it was what we needed."

"Barry walked out on Vanessa the following year," said Neil.

"Exactly," said Debbie, "it proved my point. The three of us had issues to work through. Stacey and Lucy helped the three of us cope with our losses."

"Pat's leaving wasn't much of a loss, though, from your perspective," said Neil.

"It wasn't," shrugged Debbie. "I missed my Dad and my life before I met my freak of a husband."

"You mentioned earlier that Stacey was as good as gold," said Gus. "Who was responsible for that?"

"We each played our part. Stacey knew right from wrong."

"Yet she played truant from school. There's little point denying it," said Gus "The school head, Ms Moseley, is outside, sitting with Lucy. She will confirm that fact, won't she?"

"Stacey never stayed off school when she was at home," protested Debbie.

"Who was Stacey with on these occasions? Do you have any idea?" asked Gus.

Debbie shook her head.

"I told you I was a terrible mother," she said, on the verge of tears.

"You were concerned about that, weren't you?" asked Neil. "You asked Vanessa to play down the number of occasions when the girls slept somewhere other than Gorse Hill when she spoke to the detectives."

"I *had* to spend less time with the girls; Mum and Nessie

needed them," said Debbie, "I just knew the social people wouldn't see it that way. They'd claim I was negligent."

"You couldn't risk losing the girls," said Gus, "even though you only saw them for a few hours a week in term time. Pat's regular maintenance payment helped keep you afloat as long as you could keep working. The child benefit was your spending money on a night out."

"I was a woman alone," cried Debbie.

"Maybe, but it takes two to tango," said Neil. "After Pat walked out, how long before you found a substitute for the two hours of fun he provided?"

"You make it sound dirty," said Debbie, drying her eyes.

"We've got all morning, Debbie," said Gus. "If you brought half a dozen men back to the house between Pat leaving and Stacey's death, that's six men we need to interview. If the girls came back from Mary's or Vanessa's, and one of your lovers took a shine to Stacey...."

"That's disgusting," shouted Debbie, getting up from her chair. "She was only thirteen. I never exposed my girls to anything like that. I always ensured they didn't get back until I was ready."

"Mmm, that's what we thought," said Gus, "sit down, Mrs Read. We haven't finished yet. Whose idea was it to give Stacey a mobile phone for her thirteenth birthday?"

"Mine," said Debbie. "I thought it would stop her moaning that she was the only one in her year without one."

"Mary told us she received plenty of texts and calls while she stayed at her house. Any idea who made those calls? Lads of Stacey's age from school, perhaps? Older boys from the estate had nothing to do except sell drugs to vulnerable schoolchildren. One of your lovers sat in the car outside before driving home to his wife, perhaps, and saw Stacey strolling up the street. I've seen photos of her, Debbie. Stacey looked older than thirteen and didn't dress provocatively. I've investigated cases over the past forty years where the culprit sought out exactly that type of victim. As shocking as it might sound, Debbie, that was what turned them on. So, when you leave this room, please seek out DI Francis. He's in the next room, listening in, behind the one-way glass. I need you to give him the details of every man you slept with between the day Pat walked out and the night before Stacey died."

"Then can I go to wait for Lucy?" asked Debbie.

"Just one more question," said Neil. "Why was there such confusion surrounding the arrangements for that Sunday night? Mary sent the girls home, thinking Vanessa was expecting Stacey to stay the night. Vanessa says she didn't know she was coming to stay. Why not Lucy? The girls came as a package based on everything we've heard."

"Vanessa must have forgotten, I suppose. She had her moments too."

"So we heard," said Gus. "What did you do that night?"

"I watched television, and Lucy was in bed by nine. She had school in the morning. I stayed up for a while. It wouldn't have been later than eleven when I went upstairs. I had an early start in the morning. After switching off the TV, the last thing I did was remember to dig out the change for the girl's bus fares, plus a bit extra. I suddenly remembered Stacey telling me not to forget."

"You haven't answered part of the question," said Neil. "Why was Stacey the only one sleeping at Vanessa's on that occasion?"

"Who says it was the first time she'd done it? Stacey was becoming a young woman. Lucy was still a little girl. The two-year gap that didn't bother them before became a chasm. Stacey felt more grown-up when she could stay with her Auntie Vanessa alone. It hadn't happened often; I think the first time was a month after Stacey turned thirteen. You need to ask my sister what they discussed when Lucy wasn't earwigging every word. What does it matter, anyhow? Knowing every minute of what happened, or got said on the day, won't bring Stacey back."

"The devil is always in the detail, Mrs Read," said Gus. "If we're going to unmask the person responsible for Stacey's death this time, we need to have every piece of the jigsaw. Those tiny pieces may appear unimportant, but they're vital in holding the completed picture together. That's all for now. DI Francis will collect the names and contact details of those men I mentioned earlier. Leave nothing or anyone out. The more detail we have, the better."

Debbie Read stood up and turned for the door.

"We'll interview Lucy next, Mrs Read," said Gus. "After you've finished with DI Francis, you can collect her from Reception."

"Perhaps I should stay," said Debbie.

"Lucy's head teacher, Christine Moseley, will perform the duties of a responsible adult during our conversation. I'm sure you appreciate that we must give Lucy every opportunity to speak freely about her relationship with Stacey. They would undoubtedly have had secrets that they wouldn't share with you. I'm sure you and Vanessa were the same at that age. You admitted this morning that things changed after Stacey reached thirteen. How did Lucy feel getting separated from her sister? Did she know something of Stacey's phone conversations that could prove important? If you were sitting beside her, would she feel uneasy telling us something that, if she'd spoken up at the time, could have changed how things turned out?"

"What could Lucy have known?" said Debbie. "Why wouldn't she have told me?"

"Lucy didn't want to hurt your feelings," said Neil. "Think back to that Monday morning. You cycled off to work at Dorcan. Stacey didn't arrive back from Penhill to change into her school uniform. When you spoke to that eyewitness near Redpost Drive, they told you Stacey was wearing jeans and a hoodie. It was what she wore when she left you."

"Vanessa had made sure Stacey was up and dressed, ready to catch a bus across town on the other occasions, hadn't she?" said Gus.

Debbie Read stood with her hand on the door handle and nodded.

"You weren't there to know Stacey didn't arrive in time that morning to change, collect the bus fare money from the kitchen table, and catch the school bus with Lucy. Lucy knew. She took the money and went to school alone. When Stacey wasn't at home in the evening, Lucy told you how easy it was to miss one another in such a large school. She didn't query why Stacey didn't return from Vanessa's as usual. Perhaps, Lucy knew what caused Stacey to dash off to Redpost Drive? Maybe Lucy is the key to learning why Stacey moved from where she was last seen alive to the nature reserve."

"You didn't know your daughters as well as you thought, Mrs Read," said Neil. "They both kept secrets from you. That's why we should speak to Lucy without you. DI Francis will be outside in the corridor in the next ten seconds. Concentrate on his questions for the time being."

Debbie Read resigned herself to her fate and left the

room. Thirty seconds later, Christine Moseley ushered in a timid-looking Lucy Read.

Gus recognised Ms Moseley. Tess worked for several headteachers over the years. They were teachers with long service medals that had merited the move to the top job. These days they were from the same mould. Young, politicised individuals disguised as benevolent dictators who were skilled administrators but couldn't teach for toffee.

"I hope this won't take long," said Christine Moseley. "Lucy is too young to get grilled in this manner."

"We always keep our conversations as brief as possible," said Gus, "regardless of the interviewee's age. We seek the truth. If Lucy tells the truth, she'll leave here in a few minutes. The same applies to you."

Christine Moseley sat beside Lucy Read. Gus had drawn his line in the sand.

He wanted to control this conversation. That's why he thought on his feet and handed the job of making a list of Debbie Read's lovers to Gareth Francis. No way was Debbie sitting in on this conversation. As for the head teacher, well, she needed to behave the way he'd had to when at school. Speak when spoken to and not before.

"Lucy," said Gus. "Do you know why we asked you to come here today?"

"I had to come with Mum," she replied. "There was nobody to look after me."

"Did Mum say why we wanted to talk to her?" asked Neil.

"She said it was about Stacey,"

"You must miss Stacey," said Neil.

"She was my only sister. Of course, I miss her."

"Did Stacey have a boyfriend?" asked Gus.

"No, but she knew several boys from school."

"She phoned them in the evenings, and at weekends, I suppose?" said Gus.

"No. They phoned Stacey."

"Did Stacey mention the names of the friends she spoke to?" asked Gus.

"Ryan was one," said Lucy.

"That would be Ryan Lock," said Christine Moseley.

"Thank you, Ms Moseley," said Gus. "we're aware of the young man."

"Anyone else, Lucy?" asked Neil.

"Not really. Stacey called people 'mate' or 'honey', so I couldn't tell who it was."

"Do you remember the night Stacey went missing, Lucy?" asked Gus. "Where was Stacey going, do you know?"

"She said she was staying with Auntie Nessie, but she didn't."

"Who was she going to meet? Did she say?" asked Gus.

Lucy shook her head and stared at her feet.

"Stacey just picked up her bag, got dressed to go back out in the cold, and left. She never said where she was going, I promise."

"That was the purse she carried with her money, house keys and phone. Is that right?"

"She took that, yeah, but she took a big shoulder bag too that she used to carry her school books and gym kit in."

Gus and Neil shared a glance. Debbie Read had never mentioned a missing bag. The police hadn't found a shoulder bag in the nature reserve or the canal. So whoever took the mobile phone must have taken the bag too.

"What did you do after Stacey left?" asked Neil.

"We watched telly, and then Mum said I needed to go to bed. I had school in the morning."

"Did you hear Mum come to bed?" asked Gus.

Lucy shook her head.

"I was asleep. I never saw Mum until teatime on Monday when she got home from work."

"What did you think when Stacey didn't get back from Auntie Nessie's?" asked Gus. "Weren't you scared, travelling to school on the bus alone?"

"I always sat with one of my friends," said Lucy.

"Why didn't you tell Mum that Stacey hadn't come home, Lucy? You told Mum it was easy to miss her at school, but you knew she couldn't have been there. Stacey didn't take her uniform on Sunday night, and she needed that bag to carry things she needed for the day."

"I thought she took another day off school. I hoped if I covered for her, she would help persuade Mum to buy me a phone too."

"If Stacey didn't go to her Aunt's, where do you think she went?" asked Gus. "Where would she have slept? Did she take nightclothes in her bag?"

"I don't know," said Lucy. "When we returned from Gran's, the bag was in her bedroom. Stacey fetched it while I was telling Mum what we did while we were with Gran. We baked rock cakes."

"Were there any other places Stacey stayed the night, Lucy?" asked Gus. "a girl from school maybe, at her Dad's, or somewhere else?"

"We never stayed at Dad's," said Lucy. "Stacey had never stayed at a mate's house before. Mum would have needed to know where she was going, anyway."

"DS Davis will take you to Reception to wait for your Mum," said Gus. "You've done very well, Lucy. Thank you for helping us."

Neil Davis walked along the corridor with Lucy. Gareth Francis was twenty yards ahead with Debbie Read.

"Mum," cried Lucy. "Wait for me."

Neil watched as the teenager ran towards her mother. Gareth stood back as the two embraced.

"Is everything alright, Lucy?" Debbie asked.

"I should have told you I knew Stacey might have been missing, Mum. I should have said. Please forgive me."

"There's nothing either of us could have done to change what happened," said Debbie.

Mother and daughter followed the 'Exit' signs, and Gareth Francis walked back towards Interview Room 3 with Neil.

"Did you get anything useful from the daughter," asked Gareth. "I would have liked to hear what Gus asked her, but I was making that list."

"Gus wanted you doing something useful, guv," said Neil.

"It's just as well. I took my notebook. You've heard the term, a well-trodden path, I imagine?"

"Will you have time to get it typed by the time we've finished with the head teacher, guv?" asked Neil.

DI Francis grunted and entered his office.

Neil returned to the interview room to find Ms Moseley leaving.

"Finished so soon, guv?"

"Christine kindly provided the names and contact details for the young men we were interested in, Neil. Wayne Page and Kane Hatton appear to have a clean bill of health. Both lads had excellent attendance records and were doing well in every subject, and Kane's mother was secretary of the Parent Teacher's Association. Ryan Lock,

on the other hand, got himself excluded months before Stacey's death."

"What did he do?"

"They caught him on school premises with drug paraphernalia, Neil, which includes any implement used for administering controlled substances. Namely, one hypodermic syringe, one needle, one plastic tube, a burnt spoon, and a Zippo lighter. However, Ms Moseley asserts that they found no drugs on Lock's person, nor in the locker assigned to him."

"Ryan was cute enough to have another locker," said Neil, "acquired from a vulnerable first year under duress, no doubt. Ryan was friends with Stacey Read. Lucy confirmed that her sister spoke with him more often than others at school. Does this tarnish the sensible girl image for good, guv?"

"Ms Moseley spoke highly of Stacey," said Gus. "She was a bright student who starred in the school debating team. Stacey had strong opinions over a wide range of topical matters, such as diversity and climate change."

"We need to speak to Ryan Lock, guv," said Neil.

"Easier said than done, Neil. Ryan Lock's not been seen in Swindon for over a year. I'll ask Gareth to look for him on the computer. He might have a criminal record. I asked Christine Moseley why she didn't contact the police when those items turned up during a spot check. Because they didn't recover any drugs, the police might have found it tough to prosecute the case. Ryan could have said he discovered them in the park."

"She has a point," said Neil, "they're easy to find. Gareth's working on that list from Debbie, by the way. We could pop along to his office and start the ball rolling on finding Ryan Lock."

"Once we've looked at that list to see if we recognise any names," said Gus, "I want to get hold of Pat Read and Rod Maidment. They haven't done a runner, as far as I'm aware. We'll interview them later, and with luck, Gareth will have then found Ryan Lock. Do you feel we're getting somewhere with this case, Neil?"

"Two steps forward and three steps back, guv," said Neil. "I think we've been there before. Last time, I believe you told me it's always darkest before dawn."

"Let's hope so, Neil," said Gus.

Chapter Nine

GARETH FRANCIS WAS TYPING when Gus tapped on his office door.

"How's it going, Gareth?"

"I'm halfway through the list Mrs Read supplied," sighed Gareth. "You may have difficulty tracing several of these men. Mrs Read thinks they have returned to Poland. But unfortunately, she could only provide addresses where they stayed while working in Swindon. I hope you don't mind me saying so, but you may have missed a trick."

"In what way?" asked Gus.

"What about the first six and a half years of the marriage?"

"Debbie Read implied that her husband kept her occupied," said Gus. "I suppose her appetite meant she might have seen other men during that time. Thanks."

"Did DS Davis mention the meeting between mother and daughter just now?"

"No. That meeting was in the corridor. I take it? As you

escorted Debbie Read to Reception. Neil came out just behind you. Was something said that you think is important?"

"Lucy apologised to her mother for not telling her everything. Mrs Read told her not to worry; nothing could have changed what happened. But, no, it wasn't the conversation that struck me. Lucy is a shy, fragile individual compared to her mother, isn't she? I didn't know Stacey when she was alive, but Jake Latimer mentioned that she took after her mother in height and build. Lucy favours her father, I suppose?"

"We haven't interviewed Pat Read yet," said Gus. "I'll bear it in mind."

"Have you completed your interviews?" said Gareth. "I didn't see Ms Moseley leave. I hoped to have a word."

"You would waste your time, Gareth," said Gus. "I heard her call her partner on her mobile when she left us. I think Christine and Fiona are flying to Ibiza on Sunday."

"Oh, I see. How long before you want this list?"

"How many more names do you have to type?" asked Gus.

"A dozen," Gareth replied.

"Can you do me a favour when you've completed that list? Ryan Lock got excluded from Stacey's school just before the end of 2014. Nobody knows where he is at present. I'm sure you know where to look."

"I have other duties to perform," said Gareth, "but I'll do my best."

"Thanks, Gareth. Neil and I will trot along to the detective squad room now. I want to ask Jake a couple of questions before we leave. Neil can pop back for the list before we drive back to the office."

With that, Gus left Gareth Francis to his typing.

Neil was outside in the corridor, waiting.

"All done, guv?" he asked.

"Another fifteen to twenty minutes. You can call back later. First, let's see if Jake is in."

"I've just seen him return to the squad room, guv," said Neil.

Jake looked up as Neil and Gus entered the room. The place was busy, with detectives checking details on screens and updating files from their notebooks.

"Another dawn raid?" asked Gus.

"It's Friday, guv," said Jake. "Some people are angling for weekend overtime, and the sensible ones are getting things up together so they can go home on time. So how did it go today?"

"We didn't make as much progress as I would have liked," said Gus. "Have you got a phone number for Raj Sengupta?"

"Yes, guv," said Jake, "here we are."

Gus dialled the number. He introduced himself to the cybercrime team leader.

"How can I help, Mr Freeman?" said Raj.

"When you worked on the Stacey Read case with Jack Sanders early in 2015, which of the family convinced you that the victim was street-smart?"

"I'm afraid that was the terminology I used in my notes, Mr Freeman," said Raj. "The young girl was smart and intelligent, according to her school. The family lived in Gorse Hill, a part of Swindon that has two distinct parts. Life expectancy is significantly lower on one side of the road bisecting the district than on the other. The poorer side is populated by people living on the streets and roads. The more affluent areas include avenues, drives, and ways. Jack Sanders took the information I fed him and used my 'street-smart' phrase to describe our victim and her background."

"It's been bugging us for the past few days," said Gus. "Because Stacey didn't display those qualities in real life."

"I didn't intend to confuse matters, Mr Freeman. I thought Jack would have excluded any ambiguity from the murder file."

"It's okay, Raj," said Gus. "Jack's heart wasn't in it by that time. We'll ignore it. Let's move on to Pat Read. How did he strike you?"

"The poor girl's father. I didn't sit in on that interview. Jack drafted in Theo Hickerton to replace me; I was on a computer course."

"Right, well, I reckon that's as much as you can help us with, Raj. Many thanks."

"No good, guv?" asked Neil.

"We can forget Stacey being street-smart. That was a red herring. Where is Theo Hickerton these days, Jake?"

"He hasn't risen above the transport section role he got assigned to after the massage parlour fiasco," said Jake. "Shall I call him? What do you need to know? He might not want to speak to you."

"I want to know whether he believed Pat Read fathered both of Debbie's girls," said Gus,

Jake raised an eyebrow and called his old boss.

"That came out of nowhere, guv," said Neil. "What made you think that?"

"Gareth Francis noticed a marked physical difference between the two girls. I've never seen a photograph of Pat Read. Any information I can glean before we interview him will help."

Gus and Neil listened to Jake's conversation with DI Theo Hickerton.

"Collect that list from Gareth Francis, Neil," said Gus. "I don't think Theo's much help."

"Theo reckoned they had no reason to consider the younger daughter, guv," said Jake after he ended the call. "Theo said Stacey was a junior version of Debbie. Here comes Neil. Is that it for now? Are you heading back to the office?"

"I'll call Alex Hardy in a minute. He's in charge while we're out of the office. I need to interview Pat Read today."

"I'll see you around," said Jake.

Gus and Neil returned to the visitor's car park.

"Just hang on while I chat with Alex," said Gus when they reached Neil's car.

Alex Hardy picked up on the first ring.

"Yes, guv,"

"Can we interview Pat Read while we're here in Swindon, Alex?"

"Luke tells me Read's due home from work at three o'clock," said Alex. "He's on the early shift this week."

"Ask Luke to call him and say we'll be on his doorstep waiting," said Gus.

Gus ended the call and shook his head when Neil went to unlock the car.

"I know a decent café a five-minute walk from here, Neil. We've got time to spare for a bite to eat. Bring that list of Debbie Reads' conquests with you. How many men did Gareth have to type details for, anyway?"

"Two dozen, guv," said Neil.

Gus prayed they didn't need to find many more men to interview. As he and Neil made their way to the café, Gus considered the females in Stacey's family.

Mary Bennett might be less mobile these days, but her brain was still functioning. So she put up with Debbie foisting Stacey and Lucy on her while she entertained a string of boyfriends. Luke thought Mary had done her level best to keep Stacey grounded.

Vanessa Nicholls had slipped from a responsible regular job with a building society to part-time jobs, one of which was working behind the bar at a nightclub. Vanessa admitted having several boyfriends since her husband, Barry, flew the nest. No problem by itself, but she seemed unsure whether Stacey had ever come into contact with one of them.

Debbie Read was another matter altogether. Her aim in life appeared to be to enjoy herself at the expense of other family members. Mary and Vanessa cared for her children for a significant period to free up Debbie to have fun. Stacey had been dead for over sixty hours before Debbie contacted the police.

"The pies look tasty, guv," said Neil.

Gus ordered the same meal as he had last time. Neil opted for the steak and kidney pie.

"A penny for them, guv," said Neil.

"Who do you fancy for it, Neil?" asked Gus.

"We can discount the women," said Neil. "So that leaves us with Pat Read and Ryan Lock. Or it could be Mr Nobody, the lone canoeist Stacey bumped into by the canal."

"Not much to go on, is it? Who do we have on that list, Neil?"

Neil ran his finger down the names on the first sheet.

"A few foreign names in there, guv, plus the landlord of a pub out at Wichelstowe that I recognise. The contact details for several of these suggest they worked at Dorcan."

"Did Gareth make a note of relationships?" asked Gus.

"As opposed to one-night stands, do you mean, guv?"

"No, Neil. Married or single."

"Two-thirds married, guv. Hang on, this is interesting."

"Someone we know?" asked Gus.

"The second name on sheet two is Rod Maidment, Wroughton. Single."

"Vanessa told Alex that Maidment was the only guy likely to have seen Stacey and Lucy at her place. Their relationship was more than a one-night stand."

Their food arrived, and silence reigned as they got stuck in.

"That was great," said Neil ten minutes later. "When did Vanessa say she was with Maidment?"

"Between twelve and eighteen months before Stacey died. Why?"

"I was going to call Gareth Francis to ask whether this list is a running order. Unfortunately, it's not alphabetical."

"Do we need to know which sister he slept with first?" asked Gus.

"No, but it would be good to know if the affair with Debbie came after he'd set eyes on Stacey at Vanessa's gaff. Even if it didn't, we should add Maidment's name to our 'possible' list."

"Agreed, Neil," said Gus. "I don't suppose Debbie could pinpoint dates for every one of those liaisons. We could discount several earlier ones because the girls stayed with Mary Bennett."

"True," said Neil. He ran his finger down the page to consider the remaining names. "Nobody else familiar, guv."

"Give Gareth a call, Neil. Ask whether Debbie started when Pat walked out and worked her way through until February 2015 or if it was random. She could have had a ten-year diary in that bag of hers. While he's thinking about that, ask how he's getting on in the hunt for Ryan Lock."

"Did you want a pudding, guv?" asked Neil, eyeing the selection on the board behind the counter.

"I'd enjoy a bread-and-butter pudding, Neil, but they don't make it like they did when I was a boy. You carry on. I'll have a coffee."

While Neil went to order something fattening, plus two coffees, Gus scanned the names on the sheets for himself. Debbie had slept with twenty-four men over five years. Who was he to say that was excessive or that Debbie was negligent concerning her children's care and protection? Others would decide if Geoff Mercer or the ACC thought it fitting to pass the details to the relevant authorities.

Neil had suggested the women in Stacey Read's life were innocent.

Innocent was hard to swallow, but how could either woman connect to her death?

Gus had to pin his hopes on the three men still in the frame for the murder until more evidence surfaced.

Neil returned with two coffees. His Spotted Dick would be another five minutes.

"I'll make that call now, guv," said Neil.

"Leave it ten minutes, Neil," said Gus. "I'll settle our bill while you polish off your pudding, and you can call him from the car. I want to listen in to your conversation."

Fifteen minutes later, they reached Neil's car, and he opened his door.

"It's like an oven in here, isn't it, guv?" groaned Neil as Gus joined him. "My fault for parking it in the middle of the car park where there's no shade."

Neil called Gareth Francis and asked about Debbie Read's list.

"That woman had a remarkable memory, DS Davis," said Gareth. "She spared me the details of each encounter, for which I shall be eternally grateful. But I think the list is ninety-nine percent accurate for each year involved. Mrs Read was unclear of the order in which several of them occurred. She insisted that she'd not missed anyone out."

"Gus Freeman here, Gareth," said Gus. "Did Debbie Read have any long-lasting relationships?"

"Only five of the affairs lasted longer than one or two nights. If you study the sheets closely, I indicated those by adding an asterisk after the gentleman's name. I forgot to tell DS Davis when he collected the information."

"Thanks for clarifying that point, Gareth," said Gus. "Neil wondered whether it was a performance appraisal."

"There's an asterisk by Rod Maidment's name, guv," said Neil.

"Nothing like keeping it in the family, Neil," said Gus.

Gus missed Gareth's next comment as Neil's laughter drowned it out.

"Sorry, Gareth," said Gus, "I didn't catch that."

"I have news on Ryan Lock," said Gareth. "He's in the Young Offenders Institution in Feltham, Middlesex."

"That was quick. Well done, Gareth. I'll try not to bother you again on this case. I'm sure you have other pressing demands on your time."

"Always happy to oblige," said Gareth.

Gus nodded to Neil that he had finished, and Neil ended the call. They drove to Moredon to welcome Pat Read home from another gruelling day on the Honda production line. Gus checked his watch. They still had forty-five minutes to kill.

"Gareth Francis came up trumps again then, guv," said

Neil. "He can't detect for toffee, but he's a decent researcher."

"He could do with increasing his typing speed, Neil, and for a single bloke in the twenty-first century, he's dim, wouldn't you say? Gareth was thinking of asking Christine Moseley out for a drink. He was most disappointed when I told him she'd left before he had the chance."

"I wish I'd been a fly on the wall in the corridor when he crashed and burned, guv. Unfortunately, Ms Moseley doesn't keep it a secret."

"Why should she, Neil?"

"Fair comment, guv. Gareth should pop into that nightclub in Old Town on Saturday night. He might have more luck with Vanessa Nicholls."

"Cheeky, Neil. No, don't go putting ideas in his head. Gareth can sort out his own love life. While we wait for Pat Read, let's take another look at that list. Highlight the asterisked names. We'll ask Luke to do a background check on four of those five men. We might need to add them to our list of suspects. Rod Maidment is already a likely candidate."

"The next thing we can look at is whether any of the names on this list knew Debbie Read when Stacey was two years old."

"Good thinking, Neil," said Gus. "Just because Debbie listed them here doesn't prevent any of them having slept with her between 2003 and 2008."

"We must get Luke to ask, guv," said Neil. "Had they met while Debbie and Pat Read lived together? That will reduce the number that might be Lucy's father. We need to interview Debbie Read again, too. It could have been a one-night stand, and she was never sure whether or not it was Pat's."

"What a nightmare, Neil," said Gus. "Some people make life so complicated, don't they? If people adhered to Commandments five to ten, we would be out of a job."

At one minute to three, a Honda Jazz bearing a 2018 registration arrived on Moredon Road. It pulled up in front of the garage to the left of the detached property that Pat Read had rented since leaving Debbie and the kids in Gorse Hill.

"He's come up in the world, hasn't he, guv?" said Neil. "That place looks as new as the car,"

"Pat Read earns good money at Honda, Neil," said Gus. "Even without the maintenance sum deducted by their payroll department. His neighbours say that Pat doesn't have a social life. He tends the small front garden that we can see ahead of us. Judging by the estate's layout, they've maximised the number of properties to the acre. So the rear garden too will be compact."

Gus and Neil got out of the car and crossed the road. Pat Read stood on the step outside the front door with his keys in his hand. Debbie's husband was six feet tall, slim, and neat; Gus couldn't describe him better. His modern Metallic Steel car suited him to the ground. It was bland, as was its driver.

"Are you the detectives I'm expecting?" asked Read. "I suppose you want to come in?"

"The sooner we start, the sooner we finish, Mr Read," said Gus.

Pat Read looked edgy. Neil and Gus followed him indoors.

The interior was spotless. Neil couldn't stifle a whistle of appreciation. No matter how hard he and Melody tried to keep their new-build home looking good, they were light-years from Pat Read's standard. It put even the show home on Neil's modern housing estate to shame.

"You wanted to talk about my daughter, Stacey, is that right?" said Read.

Gus sat on a comfortable chair under the window. Read stood in front of the faux fireplace.

Neil looked at Read's black leather recliner chair in the corner. No way was he sitting on that after steak and kidney pie, followed by Spotted Dick. One stain on that leather and Read would implode.

"I'm sure our colleague DS Sherman told you the reason for our visit, Mr Read," said Gus. "So, let's cut to the chase. Why did you walk out of your marriage in 2008?"

"I'd decided that married life wasn't for me," said Read. "Debbie was content to live in a tip, and I wasn't. I hated the constant noise and mess associated with young children. Finally, after six years of never achieving an acceptable level of order in the house, I had had enough."

"Why did you marry in the first place if it might irk you so much?" asked Gus.

"We'd been seeing one another for eight weeks when Debbie announced she was expecting. She'd taken me home to meet her parents for the first time the weekend before. Harry was in my ear only days after Debbie broke the news. He didn't want an unmarried mother in his house, so marriage was our only option. You know what they say. Marry in haste, repent at leisure. Well, I soon knew that feeling. Debbie trapped me."

"You must explain something to me, Mr Read," said Gus. "It's clear there was an attraction. The two of you got together at New Year and had sex on at least one occasion. Debbie was comfortable enough with how the relationship was progressing to introduce you to Harry and Mary. The marriage took place, your daughter Stacey arrived, and Debbie gave birth to Lucy two years later. Your wife told us that sexual relations continued throughout the marriage, despite how you felt about married life."

"We argued, and then we made up. So what's unusual in that?"

Pat Read looked at his watch.

"Are we keeping you from something, Mr Read?" asked Gus.

"This will affect my schedule," said Pat Read. "I should have had my first lot of washing in the machine by now. The thirty-eight-minute cycle allows me time to hoover and polish downstairs. How long did you say this would take?"

"Relax, Mr Read," said Neil. "You're not going anywhere until you've answered our questions. If you prefer to upgrade this conversation to an official interview room at Gablecross Police Station, we can accommodate that."

"So, you would have us believe that you and Debbie continued to share the same bed, despite your differences," said Gus. "If Stacey was noisy and messy and annoyed you, why risk another pregnancy?"

"We used protection," said Pat. "That failed to protect us the first time, and then suddenly, Debbie was pregnant again."

"You must have cursed your luck," said Neil, shaking his head.

"How long are you going to keep up this charade, Mr Read?" asked Gus.

"What do you mean?"

"When did you first suspect that Lucy wasn't your child?"

Pat Read's shoulders slumped.

"The dates fitted when she told me she was late," he

sighed. "I was mad as hell. How could it happen to me twice? But, then, something didn't feel right when she brought Lucy home."

"You had nothing to do with the girls, did you?" said Gus. "You didn't visit Debbie in the hospital. You never held your daughters, helped feed them, or bathed them."

"Why should I? Debbie was their mother. I provided for them by working every hour I could. They were noisy, smelly, tiny versions of their untidy mother. As Lucy grew older, it was obvious she wasn't mine. So I left not long after she had her second birthday."

"Did Debbie tell you who the father was?" asked Neil.

"I never told her the reason I left. Debbie assumed it was because I had had enough of married life in general. I haven't spoken to her since, so there was no way she could torment me with that information."

"We don't need to ask you where you were the night Stacey died," Gus said. "The police confirmed your alibi. However, I'd like to know whether you met Stacey after walking out. Did she try to get in touch with you?"

"Never," said Pat Read. "I recognised her from her school photo in the newspaper. So Stacey was mine, alright."

"How did you get on with Vanessa, Debbie's sister?" asked Neil.

"She was another reason I couldn't stick living there any longer. They're two peas in a pod, those two. Why get married if you want to live as if you're single?"

"Did Vanessa meet with other men before Barry left her?" asked Neil.

"Not so much, if ever," said Pat. "That started once he'd moved to Germany. Vanessa was always badgering Debbie to join her on nights out."

"Did they have a night on the town together frequently?" asked Gus.

"No, Debbie was too tired to have late nights back then. But, of course, once I'd left, I heard she was partying every weekend. So Mary and Vanessa had to look after the girls."

"Was there anyone you suspected was Lucy's father?" asked Neil.

"Nobody," said Pat, "I wasn't interested."

"How did you feel when you learned of Stacey's death?" asked Gus.

"Sad. I'd never cried before that day. Stacey didn't deserve to die. I know my behaviour is alien to most people, Mr Freeman, but I hadn't seen her for over seven years. Although I could see Debbie and me in Stacey's features, she was a stranger. I doubt I would have wanted to get to know her if she lived."

Gus decided that Pat Read didn't hold any information to advance their progress in the case. He felt sorry for the man on the opposite side of the room. But a jaundiced outlook on life isn't a crime.

"I don't think we'll need to talk to you again, Mr Read," said Gus. "Do you want us to contact you if we discover who was responsible for Stacey's death?"

"I hope you find the person responsible," said Pat, "but it won't serve any useful purpose. It won't change anything."

Gus and Neil returned to the car.

"The first load of washing will be on, guv. Thirty-eight minutes. Can I get us back to the office before the final spin cycle?"

"I feel like I just spent half an hour in an alternate universe, Neil," said Gus. "I imagined him as not showing any emotion under any circumstance. Almost robotic, but he cried when he learned that Stacey had died. Odd doesn't cover it. Take a steady drive back. No rush. It's going home time. We'll set things up for Monday morning and re-charge the batteries over the weekend."

"We've got a long way to go before we wrap up this case, guv," said Neil.

"You could be right, Neil," said Gus. "I'm wondering whether we're approaching it from the wrong direction."

Chapter Ten

THE DRIVE from Moredon Road to the Old Police Station took a leisurely forty-four minutes. Then, with almost the same time left in the working day, Gus elected for a rapid debrief of Gablecross and Moredon Road events after he and Neil reached the first-floor office.

The rest of the team wanted to learn what progress they had made.

"A lot of effort for not much return, guv," said Lydia Logan Barre.

"Try to focus on the positives," said Gus.

"We know where Ryan Lock is," said Neil. "Alex, can you fix up an interview on Monday late in the morning at Feltham Young Offenders Institution?"

"Luke, here's a list of Debbie Read's male companions, " Gus said. "Ignore anyone without an asterisk after their name. You should have four names to chase. I need background checks done. I'll determine whether we need an interview with any of them on Monday. You can omit Rod Maidment from your checks. He's a person of interest.

Please get in touch with him this afternoon, and we'll see him at his home near Wroughton first thing on Monday."

"On it, guv," said Luke.

Gus sat at his desk, going over the events of the past few days. What had he missed?

"We still need to talk to Debbie Read again, guv," said Neil. "Concerning the period between Stacey's birth and when she had Lucy."

"OK, we can hold off on that until Monday, Neil," said Gus. "Lydia, I want you and Alex to travel to Middlesex to chat with Ryan Lock. I'll give you a list of the answers we need."

"We'll come here first to collect your notes, guv," said Alex. "Feltham has booked us in for eleven-thirty to see Ryan Lock."

"Why was Maidment singled out as a person of interest from that list, guv?" asked Blessing. "How did he stand out from the other four names?"

"Because he was in relationships with Debbie and Vanessa Read," said Neil.

"At the same time? I can't mention that to my parents if they ask me how work went this week."

"You think you've got problems, Blessing," said Neil. "When I get home, I've got to admit to Melody that I had a Spotted Dick at lunchtime."

"Oh, Neil, you are pulling my leg. A girl brought up in the Midlands knows that you had a pudding made with suet and dried fruit, served with custard."

"I think it's time we went home," said Gus. "It's been a tough week. But, we owe it to Stacey Read to get back here on Monday, fully refreshed and ready to uncover those elusive pieces of the jigsaw that prevent us from finding the truth."

The team updated their copies of the Freeman Files, tidied their desks, and at five o'clock, Gus found himself alone in the office.

Time to make an important call.

"Mercer, speaking."

"Geoff, it's Gus here. Are you free?"

"Not tonight, Gus," said Geoff. "What about tomorrow afternoon? Will you be on your allotment?"

"Weather permitting," said Gus. "I don't think Suzie has other plans for me, although that could change when I get home in an hour."

"I'll drop by the allotments at around two o'clock. Is that okay?"

"Yes, Geoff," said Gus. "I look forward to it. It's been ages since we had a chat."

"Until tomorrow, then," said Geoff, ending the call.

Gus headed for the lift. That was the simple part done. Now he had to convince Geoff Mercer that West Mercia was a step too far. He needed him at Devizes.

Saturday, 21 July 2018

"ARE you staying in bed all morning?" asked Suzie.

"Are you leaving for Worton already?" Gus replied, opening one eye with great reluctance.

"It's a beautiful morning," said Suzie, "and I can't wait to spend it riding around the country lanes. So what will you be doing if and when you get out of bed?"

"Was there anything you wanted to add to the shopping list by the waffle maker? If not, I'll drive into Devizes, get a haircut, and then visit the supermarket. I need more picnic items for this afternoon."

"No, it's complete, as far as I remember. So you think a salmon sandwich and wine in a plastic cup will convince Geoff to stay at London Road?"

"Not on their own," said Gus. "My sparkling wit and diplomacy will win the day. The food and drink will be to celebrate a successful outcome."

"I'll leave you to recover from last night," said Suzie. "I'll be home by one o'clock."

Gus heard the front door close and the roar of Suzie's GTI as it left.

There was nothing for it. Gus knew he had to admit he wasn't as young as he was; recovery from a heavy night lasted far longer these days. They hadn't intended the evening to turn out the way it had.

When Gus had arrived a few minutes before six, Suzie had been home for forty-five minutes. The washing machine was chugging away quietly in the corner of the kitchen. Gus could hear the sound of the Dyson coming from the lounge. Someone was busy. What was the rush?

"I'm home," he called.

"Good," said Suzie, "get changed from those work clothes. I'll be starting a second wash in around ten minutes."

"A thirty-eight-minute cycle?"

"Sorry?" asked Suzie.

"I managed to look after myself after Tess died," he said. "I'm not helpless. Although, I admit I wouldn't have known the exact length of a normal wash for my machine before meeting Pat Read today. He has the same model."

"Stacey Read's father. A bit of a character, isn't he?"

"Pat Read can't bear dirt or noise. Everything in his

house was in pristine condition. I looked through the patio doors at his back garden and saw an immaculate lawn of artificial grass. I've seen the effects of time, weather, and footfall on that type of product. The only way Pat Read could keep it looking that good is if he rolled the monstrosity up and replaced it with a new patch every three months."

"I sense that you're not a fan," grinned Suzie. "I agree with you; it's naff. Okay, Pat Read might be anal, but did he kill his daughter?"

"Never in a million years," said Gus. "The only flicker of emotion I saw from the man was when he admitted that he cried when he heard Stacey was dead. I'm convinced Pat wasn't the father of Debbie's second child. If he had it in him to kill anyone, it would have been Debbie."

"That's something new," said Suzie, "tell me more while we get this house ship-shape."

Gus took Suzie through the meetings they had at Gable-cross and Moredon.

"How were things at London Road?" he asked after they finished the household chores.

"Grace Packenham continues to annoy everyone she meets," said Suzie, "I've avoided the woman so far. I felt sorry for Kassie Trotter today."

"Don't tell me. Ms Packenham isn't a fan of sticky buns," said Gus. "It would be the end of life as we know it if that tradition went."

"Grace quoted various Health and Safety legislation items to the poor girl this afternoon. Kassie said she'd had no complaints before and invited the DI to inspect her kitchen. It got heated. Geoff Mercer had to step in to prevent them from coming to blows."

"I've not met Ms Packenham yet," said Gus, "but Kassie

would make mincemeat out of most people, male or female."

"The ACC heard the commotion and stood in the doorway of his office. He expected Geoff to tell him what was happening, but Geoff disappeared downstairs."

"I'd better buy extra goodies for tomorrow afternoon. It sounds as if Geoff and I have more matters to discuss."

"Where do you want to eat this evening? Suzie asked.

"The number of items on our list suggests we have little to offer in our fridge or freezer," said Gus. "It's a takeaway or a visit to the Lamb."

Suzie pulled a face.

"We could call a taxi and eat at the Waggon & Horses," she said. "We'll be in the Lamb after our picnic at the allotment."

Gus hadn't needed to be asked twice, although this morning, he'd wished he'd been able to convince Suzie the takeaway was a better option. The food was excellent, as always, but they arrived back at the bungalow in high spirits without restricting their liquid intake. When would he ever learn?

Gus levered himself out of bed and made it to the shower. Ten minutes later, he stood in the kitchen and wondered if he should skip breakfast. Two black coffees revived him enough to brave one slice of buttered toast. He checked his watch. It was too early to risk driving yet.

When Suzie returned to the bungalow, she had found Gus unloading shopping from the boot of the Focus.

"You're cutting it fine," she said. "I thought you were meeting Geoff at two."

"How did you drive to Worton without getting pulled over and breathalysed?" said Gus. "I didn't feel safe to drive until eleven o'clock. So I decided to forgo the haircut and grab the shopping. The checkout girl thought they were recording an episode of 'Supermarket Sweep'."

"You had a nightcap when we got home last night, or don't you remember?" said Suzie.

"You had a glass of water," said Gus as he stacked the shopping bags on the worktop in the kitchen. "I wanted to continue our discussions concerning Pat Read's obsession with the clock."

Gus checked the bottle recycling bin.

"I finished the bottle of scotch," he said. "You see, I remember everything clearly."

"Because you had consumed copious amounts of alcohol, you started telling me more than I wanted to know about Debbie and Pat Read's love life. You mumbled something about forty minutes when you eventually followed me into the bedroom."

Gus groaned. Some things were best forgotten.

"I'll send Geoff a text," he said," to tell him we won't make it to the allotment before half-past two. Then, after you've changed out of your riding gear, you can give me a hand preparing the picnic. I'll get this shopping stored away."

Suzie went to the bedroom, and Gus heard the shower running a few minutes later. When Suzie returned, Gus had cleared the worktop for action. In silence, they worked side by side for thirty minutes, and then Suzie fetched the wicker basket from the hallway.

Gus began loading the food and drink into the basket. It had been ages since that slice of toast, and his appetite was back.

"Not bad," said Suzie, "we've got everything ready, and it's not two o'clock."

Suzie persuaded Gus to stroll along the lane, telling him the fresh air would do him good.

"You're quiet," she said. "What's the matter?"

"Last night, I suppose," said Gus. "I made a fool of myself, didn't I?"

"Don't be daft," said Suzie, wrapping her arms around him. "There's nothing wrong with twenty-nine minutes."

GEOFF MERCER GAVE the couple a cheery wave as he passed them by the Lamb in his car.

"Geoff looks happy enough," said Suzie.

"Maybe he's decided," said Gus. "What if he can't wait to get out of Devizes?"

"That wasn't what you said earlier," said Suzie. "You claimed your wit and diplomacy would win the day. The battle isn't lost yet."

When they arrived, Geoff was on his phone, still sitting in his car by the allotment entrance. Gus walked across to his garden shed and unlocked it. Suzie helped him retrieve the fold-up table and two chairs from inside. Gus placed the wicker basket on top of the table for later. Their first job was to get on with gardening.

"The Reverend has been busy this morning," said Suzie admiring the tidy plot next door. "I wonder whether she's writing her sermon this afternoon. Or she could be in the Lamb with Brett Penman."

"Clemency's bicycle wasn't chained up outside," said Gus as he disappeared into the shed to fetch his tools.

"Brett could have collected her from the Rectory in his car," said Suzie.

"Good afternoon, you two," said Geoff Mercer. "A lovely day for it."

"I hope that phone call doesn't mean you have to dash off, Geoff," said Gus.

"No, it was only Christine. Hark at me, only Christine. She'd kill me if she'd heard that. So why do women make such a fuss over fixtures and fittings?"

Gus swallowed hard. It was worse than he thought. He had pinned his hopes on Christine Mercer, putting her foot down regarding a move to Worcester. If she was choosing carpets and curtains, then Geoff must be past the considering stage. West Mercia would soon reveal their latest Assistant Chief Constable.

"A costly business, moving," said Suzie.

"It's been so long since we moved to a new house," said Geoff. "You forget the hassle, don't you?"

"It didn't take you long to find a place," said Gus. "That course you attended was only weeks ago. From what I remember, a move can take six months."

"What's the course got to do with it?" asked Geoff. "Christine has been in favour of us downsizing for years. So we've driven around Devizes every weekend for the past nine months, viewing different cottages. Christine finally found one she liked, and we can exchange contracts in four weeks if we're lucky."

"I thought you were leaving us to move to Worcester," said Gus. "The ACC told me that West Mercia had been after you since you attended a course where you outshone every other speaker."

"I did do rather well that week," said Geoff, "and yes, they approached me to suss out if I was available."

"What did you tell them?" asked Suzie.

"That my wife and I were perfectly happy in Wiltshire, and I hoped to stay here until my retirement. Gus reminded me earlier this year I wasn't Chief Constable material. I aspired to reach the top of the tree when I was young and foolish, but I love where I am and what I do. The family's more important at my age."

"Kenneth is still under the impression that you're mulling over whether to accept the West Mercia offer," said Gus. "One reason I suggested we meet was the ACC thinks you've been avoiding him. Kenneth told me that any meetings you attend get cut short. You stick to the agenda and make an excuse to dash off if it looks like he's going to raise another subject."

"True," said Geoff. "I'm frightened the PCC will offer me the ACC role that will become vacant when they've found a new Chief Constable."

"I thought you would jump at the chance," said Suzie.

"I would," said Geoff, "but the timing's wrong."

"You've lost me," said Gus.

"I never gave the West Mercia idea any consideration. It wasn't for me. Setting the job situation aside, Christine and I had enough to consider with the upheaval of moving looming over us for the past few months. That's why I've kept my distance. But, unfortunately, whenever I'm with the ACC, I sense he's itching to ask me whether I'm leaving."

"I think I get it," said Gus. "If the PCC called now, it would feel it was to stop you moving, not that he thought you merited it. Why do you think the PCC would do that?"

"Geoff thinks the PCC has found the right candidate for Chief Constable," said Suzie.

"He has," said Gus, handing Geoff Mercer a plastic cup.

"Where from?" asked Geoff.

"Kenneth's wife has agreed to postpone her world cruise so she can bask in the glow of her husband's elevation to the top job for a year or two," said Gus. "He told the PCC that his one caveat was that you would replace him. Kenneth insisted the team stayed together."

"The ACC has been fearing the worst," said Suzie, "when you kept avoiding him, he thought you were off to the Midlands.

Gus removed the bottle of white wine from the wicker basket.

"I shouldn't drink on an empty stomach," said Geoff.

"You can have half a cup," said Gus, "as you're driving. Then, we'll bring you a bottle when you and Christine invite us to the housewarming party."

"Where is the idyllic cottage that Christine fell in love with?" asked Suzie.

"Clench Common," said Geoff. "It's out Marlborough way and further to drive to London Road than at present, but it's perfect for when we've both retired. Christine is planning for the future."

"We intend to work on the land this afternoon," said Gus, "but we can take half an hour off to enjoy the moment."

"You carry on," said Geoff. "I promise not to sneak another cup of this wine. I will have one of your salmon sandwiches, though. You make a lot of food for just the two of you, don't you?"

Suzie laughed.

"Gus thought he'd have his work cut out persuading you to stay. He said he'd miss you."

"I never thought I'd see the day when Gus Freeman got sentimental," said Geoff.

"I never thought I'd call you a friend," said Gus, "but as I told Kenneth, my opinion of you has changed over the past months. I had to prevent you from leaving. The three of us work well together. If I had two unfamiliar faces from other areas as my superiors, the Crime Review Team would have a new consultant at the helm. We're a winning team; only a mug would jeopardise that."

Suzie and Gus tackled a few of the lighter tasks on the list for the afternoon. It was too warm to do anything too strenuous. Geoff lounged in one of the chairs and watched. When Gus looked over, there never seemed to be a time when Geoff's paper plate wasn't fully loaded. He would never change.

"Where's that old chap you keep mentioning?" asked Geoff. "The retired butcher."

Gus studied the church clock next door.

"It's a quarter past three," he said. "Bert's eighty-five, so he paces himself. On a scorching afternoon, he might sit under the apple trees in his garden, dozing. He'll arrive here around five if he thinks something needs attention on his allotment. Then, after an hour's work, Bert will reckon he's earned a pint of cider in the Lamb."

"Then he stays there, sat on a stool at the end of the bar, chatting to all and sundry until chucking out time," said Suzie.

"It's the company he craves at his age, not the cider," said Gus. "He's always got several flagons of the stuff at home. I know; I've helped him drink it."

"I ought to get going," said Geoff. "Christine will wonder where I am. She mentioned up-lighters on the phone."

"Don't run off yet," said Gus. "I said there was another item on the agenda for this afternoon. What's the story with this Grace Packenham character? Suzie told me she upset Kassie Trotter yesterday, and when I spoke with Kassie the last time I was at London Road, she said she and Vera were on staggered lunch breaks now. All in the interests of efficiency."

"Grace came highly recommended," said Geoff. "Gareth Francis got transferred to Gablecross, and at first, the PCC thought we could cope without a replacement. But the county lines cases have stretched our resources as thin as they can go without breaking."

"I could almost welcome Gareth back," said Gus. "His thinking is clearer these days; perhaps Jake Latimer is a good influence. Anything would be better than someone who's trying too hard."

"DI Packenham shouldn't trouble you, Gus," said Geoff. "Her brief is to raise London Road performance, initially in the administration section. Kenneth won't allow her freedom to interfere with our refreshments or the Crime Review Team."

"Glad to hear it," said Gus. "We must preserve Kassie's baking at all costs."

"Agreed, Gus," said Geoff. "Leave it with me. I'll ask Grace to take things easy."

"I've had a thought," said Suzie. "Now everything is out in the open; who will be in line for Geoff's position when he moves up the ladder?"

"We promote from within, wherever possible," said Geoff. "We have several DIs at London Road with varying levels of experience. The Chief Constable and his two Assistants will make recommendations to the PCC. He will be under pressure from other parties to select a certain type of candidate. Who knows which way he'll jump?"

"I don't need to ask whether you'd be interested," said Gus, looking at Suzie. "It's only a matter of time before you move up the ladder."

"I've got less experience than several of my colleagues,

Gus," said Suzie. "It's not likely that they will ask me. Grace has only been a DI for a year or two, so I wouldn't panic about finding her in Geoff's office when you report on a Monday morning."

"There's plenty of water to flow under the bridge before we need to face that decision," said Geoff. "Are you two sure you've had enough grub? I can take a doggy bag if you don't want to carry it home."

"You scoffed most of it already," said Gus. "Take the food, but leave the wine. Suzie and I can drown our sorrows. We've got to accept that you and Kenneth Truelove will still be around for a while."

"That's what you wanted all along, you crafty fox," said Geoff. "How's that latest case of yours going?"

"We have two potential suspects," said Gus, "that we're interviewing on Monday. We could tie up loose ends after that or be on the Wilts & Berks canal without a paddle. I can't quite figure out what I've missed yet."

"Well, good hunting on Monday. Despite what I've learned this afternoon, I still need the PCC to make the first move. Can you tell Vera Butler, or better still, Kassie Trotter, that Christine is shopping for up-lighters for her new cottage deep in the Wiltshire countryside?"

"I'm sure we could arrange that, Geoff," said Suzie, "leave it with me."

Geoff Mercer wrapped the rest of the food in several serviettes and walked to his car.

As he drove away, Gus and Suzie raised a plastic cup containing the last white wine.

"Let's drink to restoring the status quo for the foreseeable future," said Gus.

"Let's," said Suzie, "I like things just the way they are."

Chapter Eleven

WITH GEOFF MERCER out of the way, Gus and Suzie spent the next hour alone working on the vegetable patch. They had plenty to discuss. Geoff would soon tell Christine that, as well as the new home to look forward to; her husband was to take one last step up the ladder. They both knew Christine would be a happy bunny.

Suzie evaluated her DI colleagues from London Road to determine who would be the best fit for the Detective Chief Inspector role. Unfortunately, Gus was unimpressed with any of the names she mentioned, and Suzie accused him of being biased.

"The worst thing that could happen would be if they drafted in one of the 'woke' brigade," he muttered. "That Packenham woman is bad enough. Geoff's role needs strong leadership and management skills, which he has aplenty, but he doesn't act as SIO on cases these days. Instead, he's the lynchpin the ACC relies on to keep the various teams functioning at the highest level."

"A candidate's seniority is more valuable in the final

analysis," said Suzie. "Someone with the respect of each team leader. I suppose that's what typifies every successful team, even yours."

Gus resolved that whoever got the job would have to be someone he could respect. Frequently, he asked himself why he'd ever agreed to return to work. The cold cases intrigued him, but it would be a fruitless exercise unless his ways of working had the approval of those he reported to. This allotment would see him more often.

Kenneth Truelove and Geoff Mercer had benefitted from giving Gus his head. Unfortunately, so had several senior detectives who hadn't found answers that Gus and his team had in the past months. Three wheels were in place, but it took just one dodgy fourth wheel to make the car undrivable.

There was plenty to look forward to at London Road.

True to form, a car pulled into the gateway just as the old clock on the church tower next door gathered itself to strike the fifth hour. Brett Penman and his grandfather had arrived.

"You appear to have caught the sun, Miss Ferris," said Bert, touching the peak of his battered straw hat. "Good afternoon, Mr Freeman. My word, your patch looks a sight better than yesterday."

"It's been warm work, Bert," agreed Suzie, "I was out riding my horse early today, and we've been here since just after two, so I'm not surprised. I feel as if I'm glowing."

Bert gave Suzie a quizzical look that Gus didn't miss.

"I've kept Bert out of the heat as much as possible today," said Brett when his grandfather went to open his shed. "He needs to remember how old he is; slow and steady will benefit him these days. It's tough getting the message through that hard head of his."

"How are things progressing with the house and your job?" asked Suzie.

"I move into one of Monty Jennings's cottages next Monday, the thirtieth, and then, I start work in Wootton Bassett on Wednesday. The cottage is part-furnished. My belongings from Canada are en route but won't arrive for another five to seven days. Bert has a contact in the village whose son will help get my gear into the cottage during the day, whenever that is, so I won't need to take any time off work. I hope to get everything in its proper place next weekend."

"It will be a relief to have a place of your own," said Suzie.

"Will we get an invitation to a housewarming party?" asked Gus.

"I'm sure there will be several names on that guest list, Mr Freeman," Bert called out. "Irene and me, and the Reverend, of course."

"Where is Clemency?" asked Suzie.

"Finishing tomorrow's sermon," said Brett. "I see my grandfather's getting stuck in over there. I'd better lend a helping hand. See you later."

"Are we staying much longer, Gus?" asked Suzie.

"Have you had enough?" asked Gus. Suzie nodded.

"We had a late night last night. If we stay here, we'll join the gang in the Lamb. As much as I enjoy their company tonight, I want to chill out at home. What d'you say?"

"I've heard you call it home several times in the past twenty-four hours," said Gus. "What more could I want? The Lamb will be there another night."

Monday, 23rd July 2018

THE START of a new week dawned. Gus and Suzie felt refreshed. A quiet Saturday evening listening to music and chatting had been followed by Sunday lunch in a large family pub near Redpost Drive on the A3102 overlooking the adjoining allotments.

Suzie wondered where they were heading as Gus drove into Devizes and onto the Beckhampton straight.

"We're not going to one of our usual haunts, are we?" she said.

"Variety is the spice of life," said Gus.

After a great pub lunch, Gus suggested they take a walk. The car would be fine in the large car park for an hour. He showed Suzie the spot where someone saw Stacey Read arguing with another teenager. Then they followed the route he and Neil Davis took onto the nature reserve and the footpath beside the canal.

"Look at the number of people enjoying the beautiful surroundings," said Suzie. "Couples just out for a walk, like us. Cyclists and joggers are taking advantage of the footpath for exercise."

"Family fun at its best in an English summer," said Gus. "There were four canal trips scheduled for 'Dragonfly' today. They started at half-past ten from the landing stage at Wichelstowe. The last cruise leaves there at a quarter to three."

"How long before it sails past?" asked Suzie, looking over her shoulder.

"The trip is twenty-five minutes out and twenty-five back, so I should have timed things perfectly."

Gus and Suzie continued to walk towards the furthest

navigable point. When Gus spotted the steps leading from the road, he heard the Dragonfly's engines throb.

"Time to head back," he said, "You can wave at the passengers as they sail past if you wish."

"What a lovely sight," said Suzie. "It's hard to imagine what happened one hundred yards ahead of us three years ago. Has this second viewing helped you with the case, Gus?"

"Every little helps, Suzie," said Gus. "I couldn't see a rational way ahead when Neil and I visited the murder site. This visit has confirmed my suspicions. I'm certain no mystery canoeist or vagrant was lurking in the dark, ready to pounce on Stacey Read. Whoever was involved, they were people she knew."

"So, you're coming around to the idea Jack Sanders put forward? There *was* more than one attacker."

"It's what makes sense of where they found the discarded clothing," said Gus. "It explains the spot where they found the body and why Stacey didn't turn and run back the way she came."

"You think you know who did it, don't you?" asked Suzie.

"Not a clue," said Gus, "but I'm closer to the truth now that I've got a way in which the sequence of events could have occurred. I was going over it in my mind's eye while you admired the 'Dragonfly' as it sailed by."

"Are we heading back to the car now?" asked Suzie.

"I think we should," said Gus. "Otherwise, we'll find a quiet spot on the canal bank and stay here until sundown. It's too much of a temptation."

Gus drove them home, and as the sun blinked a final goodbye as it descended behind the trees on the distant hills, they walked to the Lamb. Some habits are more difficult to break than others.

"WHAT TIME WILL you be home tonight?" asked Suzie as they stood beside their cars in the driveway a few minutes before eight in the morning.

"I shouldn't be late," said Gus. "Good luck spreading the news about Christine Mercer's sudden interest in lighting accessories. Try to be subtle."

"Cheeky," said Suzie. "See you tonight."

Gus drove behind Suzie into Devizes and watched the GTI turn into the London Road car park. The weather was changing, with far more clouds today. Gus thought that everywhere would benefit from a good shower of rain. Unfortunately, the level in his water-butt at the allotment was lower than he'd like.

On Saturday evening, nothing had gone thirsty as Gus did the honours with the watering can while Suzie packed the picnic things and empty wine bottles into the wicker basket. He ought to stop by the allotments tonight on the way home to check nothing was suffering from a lack of rain.

Gus arrived at the Old Police Station just ahead of Neil Davis. Alex and Lydia were upstairs, and Luke and Blessing wouldn't be far behind. Gus wanted a prompt start, and the team wouldn't disappoint.

"Morning, guv," said Neil. "Another day, another collar?"

"Ever the optimist, Neil," said Gus. "Is Melody okay?"

"So far, so good, guv," said Neil. "Did you have a busy weekend?"

"Hectic on Friday evening, productive on Saturday, and potentially useful yesterday," said Gus.

"No idea how you cram it in, guv. Don't you ever wish you could put your feet up?"

"Time enough for that when I get old, Neil," said Gus as they exited the lift.

"Did you have time to prepare that list of questions for Ryan Lock to answer, guv," asked Alex Hardy.

Alex hadn't sat down since he arrived. He still held his car keys in his hand. Both Alex and Lydia were keen to get on the road to Feltham.

"I knew there was something," said Gus as he flopped into his chair. "I didn't have time to write them out. So you will have to wing it, Alex. Ask Ryan about his relationship with Stacey. Was he on Redpost Drive that Sunday night? Oh, and if he saw her that evening, was she carrying a big shoulder bag?"

"Should we ask whether he carried a knife back then?" asked Lydia.

"You can ask, but I doubt he'll answer that one," Gus said. "He's in a Young Offenders Institution for a reason. Ryan was guilty of drug offences, and many addicts carry a knife for protection. Of course, they don't necessarily use a knife threateningly, but we have known it."

"We'll get as much as we can out of him, guv," said Alex. "We should be back just after two o'clock."

"Good hunting," said Gus as Alex and Lydia headed for the lift.

They bumped into Luke Sherman and Blessing Umeh when they reached the ground floor.

"Off to Middlesex?" asked Luke.

"A fishing expedition," said Alex. "Still, it keeps us busy."

"Not as busy as last weekend," said Blessing.

"You're not kidding," said Lydia, "I know Gus asked us to recharge our batteries, but Alex took it to the extreme. So we did nothing until yesterday evening, and then I video-called my father and his partner, Rosa."

"Let's face it," said Alex. "That would have been the highlight of your weekend, whatever we'd done."

"It was satisfying to know our closeness while we were in Rotterdam hadn't faded," said Lydia. "We picked up from where we left off last Sunday evening. So what did you do, Blessing? Any more gossip about Dave you can share?"

"Dave was on nights this weekend," said Blessing. "I spoke with my mother on the phone yesterday. I almost told her I was seeing someone, but I decided it was too soon."

"You'll be okay, Blessing," said Alex. "If Dave Smith is a traffic cop, he must work various shifts in different areas of his patch. Soon, he'll get a couple of weekends free in a row, and I'm sure he'll get in touch."

"I've got nothing to add," said Luke. "This weekend did not differ from many others. Eat, drink, shop, watch TV, and sleep. Oh, we went to the cinema on Saturday night. Nicky wanted to watch 'The Outsider', set in Japan after WWII. Riveting.

"Bad luck," said Alex. "You two had better get upstairs to the office, or Gus will be on the warpath."

Luke and Blessing walked to the lift as Lydia roared away from the car park in her red Mini.

"Did Alex have his eyes closed?" asked Blessing.

"Always," said Luke.

LYDIA AND ALEX arrived at YOI Feltham in one piece.

They had forty-five minutes to kill before the eleven-thirty meeting.

"You didn't need to rush," said Alex.

"I've been to a prison similar to this with Gus," said Lydia. "It takes longer for us to get in than it has taken for several inmates to escape in the past."

Lydia was right. It was twenty-five past eleven before they reached the room set aside for the interview with Ryan Lock. Finally, on the dot at half-past eleven, a warder escorted the prisoner into the room. Ryan sat on the one metal chair on the other side of the table and stared at Lydia Logan Barre.

Ryan was seventeen, scruffy and showed little interest in being there. Lydia stared back; all she saw were tattoos, scars, and a frightened little boy behind the bravado.

"Ryan Anthony Lock?" asked Alex.

"Yeah. What's this about?"

"You were at school with Stacey Read in Swindon, correct?"

"If you've checked, you know I was, so what?"

"Stacey's mother and her aunt mentioned your name when we talked to them last week. They believed that you and Stacey were friends."

"I suppose so,"

"Remind me where it was you lived in Swindon, Ryan," said Alex.

"Juno Way. I still do. I'll be out of here in a few months."

"Your parents want you back, is that right?"

"It's only my Mum, Karen. She had me when she was still at school."

"How far is your home in Juno Way from Redpost Drive?"

"Half a mile. A five-minute walk. So what?"

"Someone saw you there together on the Sunday night she died."

"That someone needs to go to Specsavers."

"Are you sure? It makes sense, doesn't it, if you and Stacey were friends? She left home in Gorse Hill and caught a bus to Redpost Drive. Did Stacey have any other friends that lived near Juno Way?"

"I wouldn't know. What if I was there, anyway? It doesn't mean I killed her. I didn't, I swear on my Gran's grave."

"Why did she bring that large shoulder bag with her? Do you know?"

"How do I know what she had in it?"

"How often did you and Stacey meet outside school, Ryan?"

"Three, maybe four times. She kept nagging me."

"Did she disapprove of the drug-taking, Ryan?"

"A right do-gooder was Stacey. She wanted to save me from myself; that's what she said. I told her to mind her own business. If I'd listened to her, I wouldn't be here now, and...."

"And what, Ryan? Stacey wouldn't be dead? Is that what you were going to say?"

"No comment,"

"I think we can assume you were the teenage lad seen arguing with Stacey Read on the night of the eighth of February in 2015," said Alex. "Either you let Stacey walk along Redpost Drive alone to the nature reserve and her death, or you accompanied her. You're not as hard and uncaring as you try to appear, Ryan. You were fourteen, nine months older than Stacey. She was a friend, and what-ever her reason for going to Rushey Platt nature reserve that night, you wouldn't have let a friend go there alone. It was dark and bitterly cold."

"I walked with her to the bottom of the Drive. Then I walked home. Happy now?"

"Who was she meeting, Ryan?"

"I already said. How would I know?"

Lydia spoke for the first time.

"I've studied the map, Ryan," she said. "What made you use Redpost Drive, anyway? The eyewitness saw you arguing with Stacey on the other side of the road to Redpost Drive's entrance. But, if you crossed over the A3102 and walked facing the traffic back towards the pub, you could have entered Rushey Platt Park. That leads towards the canal and then through to the nature reserve."

"Stacey wanted to meet someone. They drove up Peglar's Way, and she knew he always parked near the reserve."

"I'm studying the details of your arrest, Ryan," said Alex. "There was no mention of a knife."

"I never needed one,"

"Not even that night, Ryan? Surely, you needed protection if you were venturing into a dark, lonely place such as the nature reserve."

"I wasn't carrying," said Ryan. "Stacey had a knife in her jacket pocket. That was what started the argument. I told her she didn't know who she was up against."

"So. you knew who she was meeting. Was it the drugs, Ryan?" Alex asked. "Did Stacey discover that the nature reserve was where a dealer did business? Was a thirteen-year-old girl going to confront a hardened male criminal armed with a five-inch blade?"

"No comment,"

"No need, Ryan," said Lydia. "You wouldn't have let

Stacey go there alone. You didn't abandon her at the bottom of Redpost Drive to walk home. The quickest route to Juno Way was to follow the path through the reserve and the park I mentioned."

Ryan Lock shifted uneasily in his seat and stared at the floor.

"Why don't you tell us the truth, Ryan?" said Alex.

"I can't," said Ryan.

"Let's recap, Ryan," said Alex, "to get things in the right order. Several drug-related items turned up during a spot-check at school in December that led to your exclusion. Stacey phoned when she heard the news, and you met. As a friend, she aimed to get you to stop taking drugs and discover where you were getting them. Three more meetings took place over the next six weeks, culminating in the Sunday night argument. Finally, because Stacey was determined to confront the drug dealer in the nature reserve, you walked together to the bottom of Redpost Drive and then made your way onto the reserve."

"Then I walked home," said Ryan, "I walked back through the park. I forgot. I didn't go back to the main road."

"A likely tale," said Lydia. "I think you remember every second of the night when your friend got killed."

"If you had to guess, Ryan," said Alex, "what was Stacey carrying in that shoulder bag?"

"She might have had a big torch and a blanket."

"What for?" asked Alex.

"What if she planned to lie in wait? It was freezing."

"The torch was to illuminate the face of the man she hoped to meet, I assume. What time was he arriving? How did Stacey know that was when he would be there? Did your friend realise how dangerous it could be? How could she get away?"

"Stacey was dead-set on stopping the supply of drugs to school kids. Once she got her teeth into something, she was relentless. Stacey kept nagging me to tell her when he might be in town. I phoned her in the week and told her he met someone on Sunday nights, but I never thought she'd actually go."

"We're almost there, Ryan," said Lydia. "Why don't you give us a name? Do it for Stacey and the other young lives this man is ruining."

"It's complicated. I can't say any more. He might hurt Mum if he knew I was speaking to you. If I told you anything, he'd be after me as soon as I get out. I'm sorry. I didn't want Stacey to die."

"We'll leave things as they are, for now, Ryan," said Alex. "I'll arrange protection for your mother, and as far as the outside world is concerned, you gave 'no comment' replies to every question we posed. You can contact me on this number when you're ready to talk more freely. We'll return for a full statement if we discover the person's name during our enquiries. How does that sound?"

"My Mum will be alright?" said Ryan.

"We'll do everything we can," said Alex.

"Thanks,"

The warder escorted Ryan out of the interview room. Alex and Lydia stayed behind, going over what they had learned.

MEANWHILE, in the Old Police Station office, Gus and the rest of the team spent the morning following up on the investigation's other threads.

"I'm having no luck contacting Rod Maidment on the phone number Debbie Read supplied, guv," said Luke Chambers.

"We have an address in Wroughton, don't we?" asked Gus.

"Nothing specific, guv. Debbie Read never went there. Maidment must have slept at her place while the girls were at Vanessa's or her mother's. Gareth Francis's list gives Wroughton as his location."

"Maybe Maidment got a new phone," said Neil Davis. "What about Vanessa, guv? I wonder whether her mobile number was the same as he gave Debbie?"

"There's something wrong with that list, guv," said Blessing Umeh.

"In what way, Blessing?" said Gus.

"On Friday, we asked Debbie to confirm that the list was accurate. She admitted that although several names might be out of sequence, they were correct for the year in question. I've checked the Polish nationals who no longer live in the UK. The dates when they travelled home were before the dates shown on Debbie's list. She believed we wouldn't bother checking because of the hassle of getting in touch with them."

"We're concentrating on the asterisked names on the list," said Neil, "because they were with Debbie as a couple for a longer period. What difference does it make if Debbie misremembered several one-night stands?"

"I don't believe she did, Neil," said Blessing. "I think she's moved the name of someone important and hidden the gap with these four Polish workers."

"Who could she have moved and why?" asked Gus. "What are you thinking, Blessing?"

"There are two things to consider," said Blessing. "Did

she leave a name out altogether? If we have every possible name among the four that Luke is checking, plus this Maidment character, then Debbie Read and that man have something to hide. There's something important missing between the dates where those foreign workers appeared on the list."

"Which dates do they cover?" asked Gus.

"December 2012 to October 2013, guv," said Blessing. "That's what started me wondering. It meant Debbie got lucky with four men in around forty weeks."

"That's a better strike rate than I ever managed when I was single," said Neil.

"The thing is, Debbie gave us twenty other names to cover the remaining three hundred weeks between her husband walking out and her daughter's death."

"You might read too much into the numbers, Blessing," said Luke. "One in ten, or one in fifteen, how does it help us?"

"I think Blessing has hit on something worth pursuing," said Gus. "Although I agree, there could be a simple answer. One of Debbie's girls could have been ill, and Debbie didn't get out socially for a while. Then there are the extended relationships. What if one of those men broke up with her and Debbie got hurt? She might swear off men for a month or two. Luke, take Blessing with you and interview Debbie Read again. Ask whether there was another name that she tried to hide. Show her the evidence we've gathered on the foreign workers. She might claim she got them out of sequence, but keep at her. She's hiding something. How significant it is, I don't know."

"On it, guv," said Luke.

"Neil," said Gus, "call Vanessa Nicholls. She should be out of bed by now. Check Rod Maidment's phone number.

Ask if she knows his address in Wroughton. Don't tell Vanessa that we know he also had a relationship with her sister."

"I get it, guv," said Neil, "if I ask the right questions, she might let on that she knew. I'll try to sound as if it was news to me."

Blessing thought that the morning had gone well. Something told her the anomaly she'd spotted was important. It felt good to contribute positively to the team's effort.

"Do you have anything else, Blessing?" asked Gus.

"No, guv. What do you wish me to do? I can fetch you a coffee."

"I'll go, Blessing," said Gus. "I need to keep in your good books. You did a deep dive into those four foreign workers. Can you double-check the names, addresses and phone numbers of the fifteen men you haven't looked at yet? If you're right, and Debbie Read was devious when compiling that list, she might have given us more duff information."

"Leave it with me, guv," said Blessing.

"No reply from Vanessa Nicholls, guv. I'll try again in thirty minutes. My turn now with a fact that might need checking, guv," said Neil. "When we were by the canal the other morning, we saw the cross Debbie and her sister left in memory of Stacey. Does Vanessa Nicholls drive?"

"Alex didn't make a note of a car on the drive when they interviewed her," said Gus. "I'm looking at his Freeman Files update. Vanessa told Alex that Rod Maidment drove a new Honda when she knew him. She complained of having to walk to her mother's house on Tuesday night to see whether Stacey was there. When could they go to the nature reserve together? Debbie has worked the morning to mid-afternoon shift at Dorcan since 2015.

Vanessa started working part-time before that and has supplemented that with bar work in pubs and clubs. They would need to take Lucy with them at the weekend because Mary hasn't seen her much since Stacey died. I can't see many opportunities to go together to lay flowers or leave a birthday card."

"Public transport in Swindon is excellent," said Blessing, "that's what we've learned. Debbie cycles to work each day. How long would it take to cycle to the murder site?"

"Around fifteen minutes," said Neil, checking the street map.

"How would Vanessa get there by bus?" asked Blessing.

"In forty-five minutes, with a couple of changes," said Neil. "It's doable, but Vanessa would moan because, once again, she does the hard work while Debbie cycles along the path from Rushey Platt Park right to the site of the murder."

"Any luck, Luke?" asked Gus.

"It surprised Debbie to hear from me, Guv. She couldn't understand what more she could tell us. I'm ready to leave for Gorse Hill as soon as Blessing is."

"I'm ready now," said Blessing,

"Sorry," said Gus. "I forgot your coffee. I got distracted."

"That's okay, guv," said Blessing. "The case is more important."

Chapter Twelve

LUKE AND BLESSING arrived in Gorse Hill at ten-forty. Debbie Read answered the door before Luke could ring the bell and asked them to be quiet. Lucy was still in bed in the room directly above the hallway. They followed Debbie into the kitchen at the rear of the property.

Luke told Debbie Read who he and Blessing were.

"What is it this time?" she asked.

"We're still trying to find your daughter's killer," said Luke.

"Surely, you want to help us in any way you can?" said Blessing.

"It was only yesterday you dragged us across the other side of Swindon," moaned Debbie.

"Perhaps," said Luke, "but my colleague spotted discrepancies in the information you supplied to Inspector Francis." Debbie looked daggers at Blessing Umeh.

Blessing smiled back.

"I told that detective I might have got names mixed up," shrugged Debbie. "So what?"

"Are you sure you didn't leave anyone out?" asked Luke.

"I didn't think I did. I cannot see what my private life has to do with Stacey's death."

"Maybe nothing," said Luke, "maybe everything. The dates for the foreign workers are wrong, but you know that, don't you, Mrs Read? They were back in Poland before you said you slept with them. We checked with the landlords of the properties where they stayed and then checked the flights they took to Krakow and Warsaw. That's ten months unaccounted for, and we need the names that should appear on the list at those times."

"I don't keep a diary," said Debbie.

"We can wait while you compile a revised list," said Luke. "Here's a copy of the original."

"Before you put your thinking cap on, Mrs Read," said Blessing, "does Lucy have a bicycle?"

"Yes, why?"

"When was the last time you and Lucy cycled from here to Rushey Platt?"

"I don't believe we've ever put her through that ordeal," said Debbie. "I've gone with my sister. I cycle across, and Nessie gets the bus."

Luke heard Lucy moving around upstairs.

"That sounds like Lucy, Mrs Read," he said. "Would you mind if we asked a few questions while you concentrated on that list?"

"Yes, I would mind. Lucy got most upset yesterday when she had to go through it again."

"We'll leave it for another time," said Luke. "My colleague will sit with her in another room, but there will be no questions, okay?"

"Can I trust her," asked Debbie, looking at Blessing.

"Of course. It would save valuable time if you admitted

who you saw between December 2012 and October 2013," said Blessing.

"Rod Maidment, alright. It was Rod. He works at Honda. I met him again in the run-up to Christmas. We saw one another for a while before."

"When exactly?" asked Luke.

"Mum. Who are these people?"

Lucy had crept downstairs and now stood in the doorway.

"The police had more questions, darling. I won't be much longer. Sit in the front room with this lady. You can get your breakfast in a tick."

Blessing followed Lucy Read along the hallway.

"Carry on," said Luke when Lucy was out of earshot.

"The date I gave the detective was wrong. It was eighteen months after Pat left."

"So, you had a relationship with Rod Maidment at the beginning of 2009. Then you met up again at the end of 2012, correct?"

"Yes," said Debbie.

"Where was he working in January 2009?"

"Honda,"

"Has he worked there continuously from the time you met?"

"Yes,"

"Why don't you know his address in Wroughton?"

"He never took me there."

"How do you know he wasn't married? Perhaps he has a wife and children. Unfortunately, we can't get hold of him on the number you provided. Why is that?"

"I haven't spoken to Rod since we stopped seeing one another. I suppose he swapped phones, so I couldn't get in touch."

"Do you know who he started seeing after he ended things?"

"No idea," said Debbie, "they're welcome to him."

"Do you know anyone Vanessa might have seen during that period?"

"It was never something we discussed. Nessie and Mum weren't happy with my lifestyle. I needed company after Pat walked out. I didn't want them poking their noses in my business, so I kept out of theirs. Why? How do my sister's men friends have anything to do with Stacey?"

"Stacey was an attractive young girl," said Luke. "You know what the police thought could have happened. Her attacker didn't set out to kill her. Their initial motive was sexual. Stacey ran, got stabbed, fell into the canal, and drowned. We believe she knew the man, or at least the man knew her. Perhaps his name is on that list you're holding, Mrs Read. Or maybe, one of Nessie's lovers spotted her when your daughters arrived earlier than planned one weekend. Is there anyone on your list that your sister might have known?"

"I don't know. Do I have to ask her? I'm not sure either of us would want to know."

"Do you want Stacey's killer brought to justice or not?" asked Luke.

"I suppose I have to then, don't I?"

"How did you get to Redpost Drive that night when you were searching for Stacey?"

"I cycled to every likely spot I could think of," said Debbie. "That dog walker was the only person I spoke to who had seen Stacey."

"Where did you go after you spoke to the lady with the dog?" asked Luke.

"I cycled home. It was cold. There wasn't anyone on the

nearby streets to ask, so I came back here. I hoped I'd find Stacey on the doorstep, saying she'd lost her keys and phone."

"Run through the list again, Mrs Read," said Luke. "Adjust for any errors you spot. I'll fetch Lucy and my colleague. We'll let you get on with your day. If we need more information, one of the team will be in touch."

Ten minutes later, Luke and Blessing were in his car.

"Did Lucy ask questions, Blessing?"

"The usual; why were we there? Was her Mum in trouble? Nothing more. How did you get on with Mrs Read?"

"She admitted to two extended relationships with Rod Maidment,"

"Does she know he went straight to Vanessa's bed after ending it with her?"

"Not a clue unless she's an exceptional actress. I hinted that she should check to see whether they had a lover in common. I pointed out that Stacey could have been the target of a sexual attack from one of her ex-lovers or one of her sisters' boyfriends."

"That must have horrified her," said Blessing.

"No, and that was the crucial snippet I took from our conversation, Blessing. I need to make sure Gus hears it. Debbie Read was more concerned about asking her sister if they'd slept with the same man than she was about one of their lovers taking a shine to her daughter and attempting to rape her."

"Debbie Read is a cold, heartless woman," said Blessing, "only concerned with her own gratification. Did you ask who Lucy's father was?"

"No, I didn't. I wasn't sure how Debbie would have reacted, and you had Lucy in the other room. Lucy needs to learn the truth one day, but today was not the day. Gus should decide how we handle that knowledge."

"We haven't got definitive proof yet," said Blessing.

"Let's get back to the office," said Luke, "and wait for Alex and Lydia to report back from Feltham."

"I have to slog through those other names on the list for Gus," sighed Blessing.

"My checks on the four men Debbie saw for two or three weeks won't take long," said Luke. "After that, I'm not sure which way we turn."

"Until we locate Rod Maidment," said Blessing.

Luke drove them back to rejoin Gus and Neil in the office.

"How was the delectable Debbie," said Neil as they exited the lift.

"Worth a closer look," said Blessing.

Luke went through the conversation, step by step, without commenting on the impression he had gained. Blessing added the few words that Lucy had spoken into the mix.

"How long were you in there?" asked Gus.

"Ten minutes, guv," said Blessing. "She's coming up to her fifteenth birthday. I told Lucy what she needed to know. Debbie didn't want Lucy questioned under any circumstances, so I left Lucy to flick through her phone. She was just browsing. She didn't send or receive any messages."

"Alex and Lydia should be back in an hour," said Gus. "I'll digest what you've discovered. In the meantime, update your Freeman Files, carry on with the research you started earlier, and we'll reassess where we are after we learn what Ryan Lock offered."

"I've updated my files, guv," said Neil, "what can I do to

help? I'm seeing Vanessa Nicholls later this afternoon. I don't need to leave until four."

"Neil could widen the search for Rod Maidment, guv," said Luke. "We know from Debbie that he worked at Honda in 2009, and he's still there as far as we know. So maybe Maidment gets a new car yearly, the same as Pat Read. But, unfortunately, we have nothing on him apart from the name. No photo or home address. No description or car registration. Is he on social media? Are there photos online of him, his friends, and his car? He's a mystery man."

"There you go, Neil," said Gus. "Get your teeth into that."

"Should we concentrate on identifying Lucy's father, guv?" asked Blessing. "I know that it only takes one time to get pregnant, but isn't it more likely to be someone Debbie was with for an extended period?"

"We didn't ask Debbie about any men she went with when she was living with Pat Read, guv," said Luke. "I didn't raise the subject this morning because we've said throughout that Debbie had no connection to her daughter's death."

Gus sat back in his chair. *What was it he said to Neil that day by the canal? We might be coming at this from the wrong direction. Was that it?*

"I'll add those thoughts to my deliberations while we wait for the others," he said. "Let's hope they bring back the final missing pieces."

He's nearly there, thought Neil. *I can see the cogs turning more quickly. I wish he'd share his thoughts with us because I'm as much in the dark as I was when we started.*

Luke was thinking of Debbie. After Stacey left, Debbie said she watched TV with Lucy until her daughter went to bed. Lucy confirmed that was what happened when Gus talked to her with Christine Moseley. When Lucy got up for school the following day, her Mum had already cycled to work. Lucy couldn't have known whether her mother left the house once she fell asleep a few minutes after nine. The eyewitness saw Stacey before eight on Redpost Drive. Who said it was nine o'clock that Lucy went to bed? Luke checked the Freeman Files for the conversation between Gus and Lucy. Nobody mentioned the time. Debbie Read had told them that was the time Lucy went to bed. Did that mean Debbie didn't have an alibi?

Blessing Umeh was ploughing through the fifteen men's details with whom Debbie Read admitted having a one-night stand. It proved boring and unproductive. Her mind drifted to Debbie Read cycling around Swindon. Cycling is an excellent way to keep fit.

Lucy had a bicycle too. Where was Lucy on Tuesday evening when Debbie went looking for Stacey? Vanessa didn't have her, nor did Mary, her grandmother. She was at bingo in Greenbridge. Had Lucy gone with her mother? She never mentioned it to Gus. What time would they have left home, and how long did they search?

Blessing abandoned the laborious checks and plotted a route that mother and daughter might take.

Alex and Lydia came through the lift doors at five minutes to two.

"Did you have your eyes closed for the entire journey, Alex?" asked Luke.

"I deserve a medal, Luke," said Alex, "it was the definition of a white-knuckle ride."

"I couldn't wait to get back to tell you what we found out," said Lydia.

"We're listening," said Gus.

"Ryan Lock and his mother, Karen, live off Juno Way,

five minutes from Redpost Drive," said Alex. "Ryan caved after a few minutes and admitted that he was the lad seen with Stacey that night. She had a heavy blanket in the large shoulder bag to protect herself against the cold. She planned to lie in wait for a drug dealer arriving via Peglar's Way at around eight-thirty. The man supplied several kids from Stacey's school. Ryan told Stacey what time the dealer would be there. Stacey planned to take a photo of the guy, illuminated by a large torch she had in the bag, and hand it over to the police. Ryan told us the argument began when he realised Stacey had a knife."

"Ryan is just a frightened kid," said Lydia. "He warned Stacey that she didn't know what she was up against confronting this man. We kept pressing him for more information, but he feared for his life and his mother's. Alex has promised to get protection for Karen Lock. She's only in her early thirties, guv, and a single mother. Ryan told us she had him while at school."

"Another schoolboy was the father, or someone older, perhaps this drug dealer?" asked Gus.

"Ryan didn't say, guv," said Alex. "I gave him a card and asked him to call when he's ready to talk. When I said we'd come back if we discovered the man's identity ourselves, he agreed he would give us a full statement."

"Provided his mother was safe," said Lydia.

"Where's Peglar's Way?" asked Gus.

"Before we got to the bottom of Redpost Drive the other morning, guv," said Neil, "we cut through to the nature reserve. The road dead ahead of us was Peglar's Way. This dealer could have come from Wichelstowe, East Wichel, or anywhere at that end of town. They could have come from anywhere if they know their way around."

"Was there anything else, Alex?"

"Those were the highlights, guv. I'll enter the full script into the files now."

"Okay, Alex," said Gus, "you do the same, Lydia."

"On it, guv," said Lydia.

"Right, listen up, everyone," said Gus. "Our priorities are as follows. First, interview Karen Lock and arrange protection. Second, contact Gablecross for names of dealers active over a long period in that part of Swindon. Who is this thug Ryan Lock told us Stacey was waiting to intercept. Third, analyse what Neil gets from Vanessa Nicholls on Maidment, including any social media content. Then we should detain Rod Maidment and interview him."

"There could be someone else involved, guv," said Blessing. "Whoever the dealer is, he wouldn't hang around on a freezing night on the off chance somebody wanted to score."

"The guy was expecting someone, you mean?" said Gus.

"Is it possible, guv?" asked Blessing.

Gus clicked his fingers.

"That's why Stacey kept running away from the exit to Redpost Drive."

The rest of the team exchanged glances.

"Luke, can you get hold of Karen Lock, please," said Gus. "We'll set the wheels in motion straight away."

Gus picked up the phone and dialled.

"Rick, Gus Freeman here. Are you involved in something major? No? If I call your boss, do you think there's a chance he'd free you up for surveillance work over the next three or four days? Good. If he agrees, I'll see you in the office first thing tomorrow."

"Is Rick Chalmers returning to the fold, guv?" asked Neil.

"An extra body will help. Each of us will take a share of the load, Neil," said Gus. "We must continue with the spadework we've got underway, and then it's a case of watching and waiting."

"Karen Lock's at home, guv," said Luke. "I can drive over with Neil if you wish. We can go directly to Vanessa Nicholls after talking to Ryan's mother."

"Excellent," said Gus. "Ask Karen for a photo of her with Ryan as a child. Get the name of the father if she knows it. Follow your nose. You'll know what to ask."

"Right, guv," said Luke, "ready, Neil?"

"Born ready, mate."

When they were in the car park, Neil turned to Luke.

"Gus has got it sussed, hasn't he? I wish I could see the complete picture."

"What if Debbie Read doesn't have an alibi for Sunday night, Neil?"

"You can't believe it involved her, Luke. Debbie was home with Lucy."

"What if Debbie sent Lucy to bed early that night?" said Luke. "I can't see where Lucy mentioned the time anywhere in the files. Debbie told Gus it was nine and that she went to bed at eleven."

"What makes you think she's capable? Ryan Lock confirmed it was drug-related. Stacey was hoping to foil a drug deal in the nature reserve. It's odds-on that if anyone else entered the reserve that night, it was a junkie."

Luke drove them out of town and made for the Wootton Bassett road into Swindon. He continued to mull over the facts they possessed, trying to fashion a viable solution. It was one of Gus's jigsaw analogies. They had a piece that appeared to fit but needed to get moved for the remaining pieces to gel.

Once on Juno Way, it was only two minutes before Luke knocked on Karen Lock's door.

"Mrs Lock? DS Sherman from Wiltshire Police. My colleague is DS Davis. Can we come in?"

Karen Lock nodded and stood aside as the two detectives entered the hallway.

"In here," said Karen, "sit yourselves down. What was it you wanted to know?"

"Our colleagues visited Ryan today," said Luke. "He's concerned for your safety."

Karen Lock looked nervous. Her hands shook as she grabbed a pack of cigarettes and a lighter from the table.

"My safety? What's he been saying?"

"I think it's time to speak out, don't you, Mrs Lock?" said Neil.

"Ryan's dead if he's talked. He wouldn't. You're fishing. I won't go against him."

"Who, Karen," said Luke, leaning forward. "Who's got the two of you so scared?"

"We can protect both of you, Karen," said Neil. "The wheels are in motion. You just have to cooperate, and we'll take care of everything."

"That man has made my life a living hell for eighteen years," said Karen. "Ryan would have stayed honest if that brute hadn't come back. Once he got his claws into Ryan with the drugs, he manipulated him any way he wished."

"Ryan's in a better place now, Karen," said Neil. "He's getting help. But, if you want him to stay free of this man for good, tell us what you know."

"We're talking of Ryan's father, aren't we, Karen?" said Luke. "A man who got you pregnant when you were fourteen or fifteen?"

Karen Lock nodded and took a long drag on her cigarette.

"I was fourteen and a half when it happened. I was in town with my friends in a café, just killing time. We skived off school most afternoons. He was in there every day. One time he offered to take us home. He dropped off my mates one by one, and I was alone with him. He wouldn't let me out of the car."

"Did he rape you, Karen?" asked Neil.

She nodded.

"Why didn't you report it?" asked Luke.

"He told me what would happen if I did," said Karen. "I had a younger sister. Then a few months later, I realised I was expecting. And he was gone. I never saw him again for years."

"This was in 2000, is that right?" asked Neil.

"In the spring, yeah,"

"Give us Ryan's father's name, Karen," said Luke.

"I can't. He came back, and he's got eyes and ears everywhere. If you go near him, he'll know it was me. He won't rest until he's finished both of us. He's an animal."

"We'll arrange for this place to be watched twenty-four-seven," said Luke. "Protection is already in operation at YOI Feltham. We'll do everything we can to identify this man and get him behind bars."

"I hope you do. I'd love to live my life without looking over my shoulder."

"Do you have a photograph of you and Ryan when he was a baby?" asked Luke.

Karen nodded towards a bookcase behind him.

"There are several in that larger picture frame. You can take one if you promise to bring it back."

"We will," said Luke.

"Do you have any photos with Ryan's father in them?" asked Neil.

"Nothing," said Karen.

"Give us a description," said Luke.

"He was around thirty back then. A little under six foot tall, dark hair, heavy build, and he had a scar an inch long on his left cheek, close to his mouth."

"Any tattoos?" asked Neil.

Karen Lock shook her head.

"Call if you change your mind about giving us his name," said Neil. "It would help you both move on so much faster."

"When I know Ryan's safe," said Karen.

Neil and Luke left Juno Way and drove to Penhill. Vanessa Nicholls was walking along the street as Luke parked the car.

"Perfect timing, Mrs Nicholls," said Neil. "Let's get on with it, shall we?"

Vanessa Nicholls let them in, walked into the front room, flopped onto the settee and looked at Luke and Neil.

"What is it now?" she asked. "I've just finished work. I'm shattered."

"We tried to get hold of Rod Maidment using a number from another witness," said Luke. "It appears to be incorrect. Can you give us the number you used to contact him?"

Vanessa fished in her bag for her phone and scrolled through her contacts.

"There it is," she said, showing the screen to Neil.

"Thank you," said Luke. "Do you have an address for him in Wroughton?"

"No. I never went there."

"He drove a new Honda when you knew him. Is that right? What was the registration?"

Vanessa closed her eyes and tried to reel off the letters and numbers.

"It was something like that, a gold-coloured car."

"Do you know how long he's worked at Honda?" asked Neil.

"Oh, since the early 2000s. Why the interest in Rod? I haven't seen him in ages."

"Were you ever linked with him on social media?" asked Luke.

"He didn't get involved with that stuff, nor do I," said Vanessa.

"We're trying to find photos of him or his cars," said Neil.

"He didn't enjoy having his photo taken back then."

"Description?" asked Luke.

"Tall, dark, and overweight," said Vanessa. "I said that the first time you lot interviewed me. Rod told me he used to be fit but put on weight after stopping playing sports. He was talking about trying to lose weight before we finished. Then, one day, months later, I saw him when I took the bus to meet Debbie at Rushey Platt. Rod was thinner, but he still had the beard."

"Any distinguishing marks?" asked Neil.

"Rod loved a tattoo," said Vanessa, "he had a dragon on his back and a hardcore sleeve on his left arm."

"Any idea how old he was?" asked Luke.

"Not sure, somewhere between forty-five and fifty. Rod was older than me, for sure."

"Thanks, Mrs Nicholls," said Luke. "That's it for now."

"I hope so. It's not much fun talking about your mistakes in public."

"Rod Maidment was a mistake?" said Luke. "I thought you were together for several months?"

"There was something off with him," said Vanessa. "Rod could be controlling, and he never gave much away. But, as you said, Rod had his secrets. I never knew a thing about where he was in the days between dates. The physical side was good, so I ignored the secrecy."

"I don't think there's anything else, Mrs Nicholls," said Luke. "We'll let you relax for a while. No doubt you're working tonight?"

"There's nobody else bringing money into this house," she snapped. "I have to work to live."

Luke and Neil arrived back to an empty office. It was gone half past five.

"We should update our files before we leave," said Luke. "If Gus gets Rick on board first thing, the more data he has available, the better when reassessing our strategy."

"I'll phone Melody and tell her I'll be an hour," said Neil.

"Nicky will blow a fuse," said Luke. "We had a squash court booked."

Tuesday, 24 July 2018

THE TEAM FELT a different vibe in the office as soon as they arrived. Gus was first upstairs, and Alex and Lydia found him poring over the Freeman Files. Blessing Umeh soon joined them, and Gus told them what Luke and Neil had learned.

When Luke and Neil came through the lift doors a couple of minutes later, they weren't alone.

"We found this waif and stray in the car park, guv," said Neil.

"Well done, Rick," said Gus, "how long have we got you with us?"

"I'm needed back at the weekend, guv. Four days tops."

"That should be plenty, Rick. Find a chair, and I'll bring you up to speed."

Rick grabbed a visitor's chair and sat next to Blessing.

Just as Gus was going to speak, two phones rang. Gus and Alex picked up.

"How are you settling in?" Rick Chalmers asked Blessing.

"It's what I wanted to be doing," she said. "Making a difference."

"I can tell you're new," laughed Rick. "The novelty will wear off."

Blessing hoped that wouldn't be for a long time yet.

"That was Jake Latimer at Gablecross," said Gus when his call ended. "We asked him for details of drug dealers operating in the area surrounding Rushey Platt over the past decade. There's a long list, as you can imagine. But, unfortunately, Jake couldn't link anyone on his radar to the description Karen Lock supplied."

"A name might help, guv," said Alex. "That was Karen Lock on the phone. Ryan must have spoken to his mother yesterday evening to tell her to trust us. He agreed that she could tell us his father's name. He's James Neville, 'known as 'Jammy'. According to Karen, Neville was unemployed when she met him in the café but was waiting to start a new Swindon job."

"Neil, can you get back to your mate, Jake, and ask him for details on this James 'Jammy' Neville? Find out where he is, so we can get him nicked. If Ryan's telling the truth, then Neville was the man Stacey was waiting to confront."

"Where do you want me to start, guv?" asked Rick.

"At the Honda factory, Rick. We have a description of Rod Maidment from Vanessa Nicholls and an approximate registration for the gold Honda car he drove at the end of 2013. We won't go barging into Reception and ask to speak to him. I don't want Maidment alerted to our interest. I'm unsure how he connects to the case, but I'm hedging my bets. At the next shift change, we need someone to tail Maidment to this mystery address in Wroughton. The description is your best bet, plus the gold colourway. Maidment sounds like a creature of habit, so although he's probably on a later plate, we have a reasonable chance of finding him quickly."

"When is the next shift change?" asked Rick.

"Two o'clock, guv," said Neil. "They have operatives on a three-shift pattern, six to two, two to ten and ten to six. There's also a two-shift pattern that Pat Read is on, which starts at five forty-five and finishes at two forty-five. So this week Pat will do three to midnight."

"There you go, Rick," said Gus, "Six opportunities to clock Maidment between now and midnight."

"I'll get over to Swindon ready for two o'clock," said Rick. "What do I do when I've identified him and confirmed his address, guv?"

"Call me," said Gus. "We'll get another body out there to run surveillance. I want to know what he's up to when he's at home."

"Who's next, guv?" asked Neil.

"Debbie Read," said Gus. "You can drive out to Dorcan this afternoon and follow her back to Gorse Hill."

"She'll be cycling, guv," said Neil.

"Be inventive, Neil. I want to know whether she cycles straight home. Please make a note of everything Debbie does until you see the light go out in her bedroom. Understood?"

"Yes, guv," said Neil.

"Who's looking after Juno Way, guv?" asked Luke.

"Jake Latimer has people assigned to that duty," said Gus. "When he gets an address for James Neville, we'll get you to sit on that to gather information on where he does his dealing and who else might be involved."

"Are we approaching the endgame, guv?" asked Lydia Logan Barre.

"It's getting closer every day, Lydia," said Gus.

Chapter Thirteen

Wednesday, 25 July 2018

GUS DROVE into the Old Police Station car park at eight forty-five. Perhaps their luck would change today.

Jake Latimer had searched high and low for James 'Jammy' Neville but couldn't find him.

"We don't catch all of them," he said when he contacted Gus with the news. "Karen Lock met Neville in 2000, and he was unemployed. What's saying he hadn't just moved to the area for work? When he learned she was pregnant, he did a runner."

Gus had stressed to Jake that Karen reckoned Neville made her life miserable for eighteen years. Jake asked whether he tormented her in person or from a distance. Gus had phoned Karen Lock, and she told him that once Neville discovered where she lived, he sent the occasional card reminding her he could get to her whenever he pleased.

Neville first approached his son Ryan outside the school when her boy was twelve. Karen hadn't seen Neville in person since 2001 but knew through Ryan that he looked older and hairier than when they first met.

Jake concentrated on the period between 2013 and 2015. Ryan was using drugs between those dates. Stacey Read had started her campaign to get him to stop in the autumn of 2014, but Jake still came up empty.

"Neville didn't work for any of the usual suspects," he said. "He must have been a small-time solo operator who never came to our attention."

RICK CHALMERS HAD STUDIED faces and vehicles at the Honda factory throughout the day. It was impossible to cover staff leaving at two forty-five and the three o'clock arrivals. He'd not given Gus any good news before the team went home. He reported just before five to remind Gus that gold appeared the most popular colour for the cars on site. A model number would narrow the field. Gus tried Vanessa Nicholls after he got home from work, but she didn't reply. He'd left a message.

NEIL HAD SAT in his car and watched staff leaving the Royal Mail site in mid-afternoon. Debbie Read sailed out of the exit on her bicycle, wearing a helmet and a hi-viz jacket. Neil waited for two minutes and then followed. The traffic volume slowed him sufficiently, so he didn't catch her more than once. Finally, Neil overtook her and stopped in a lay-by, pretending to be on the phone until she passed him. He studied the panniers on the back of her bicycle. There might be something in them, but it might just be her wet-weather gear and her lunchbox.

When they reached Gorse Hill, Neil parked fifty yards

away from the house and kept watch. Nobody left the house, and nobody arrived, so Neil drove home at ten o'clock.

RICK CHALMERS STRUGGLED to stay awake by midnight, but he revived once he spotted a golden bronze metallic Honda CR-V with a tall, thin, bearded driver nudging fifty years of age. Rod Maidment was working three to midnight this week.

Rick followed him beyond Wroughton to a spot between there and Broad Hinton. Rick couldn't follow the car when it turned off the main A361 road but watched when the rear lights disappeared. He waited five minutes, switched off his lights and ventured into the lane.

Rod Maidment lived in a dilapidated smallholding with three outbuildings of various sizes. Rick decided it was time for bed. He would report to Gus in the morning.

Gus had the team organised for the following two days by ten o'clock. Luke, Neil, and Alex would sit on Rod Maidment with the help of Rick Chalmers.

Thursday–Friday, 26 to 27 July 2018

THE FOUR DETECTIVES tailed their man to and from work and noted everything they saw from Rick's vantage point while Maidment was home. He didn't know they were watching him. When they reached the end of the working day on Friday, their sum of helpful information was negligible.

"He's been nowhere, and he's met nobody, guv," said Rick.

In Gorse Hill, Blessing and Lydia had spent hours keeping watch on Debbie Read.

Gus Freeman followed Debbie out to Dorcan and home again. The Friday afternoon ride took eight and a half minutes longer than the average Tuesday, Wednesday, and Thursday trips. There was no change in the weather.

Gus wasn't unhappy with the limited amount of information they'd gathered. After they had said their goodbyes to Rick Chalmers, Gus took the team through the next steps.

"Okay, is everyone clear on what they have to do?" he asked.

"Yes, guv," came the reply.

Sunday, 29 July 2018

NEIL COLLECTED Gus from the bungalow at eight o'clock, and they drove towards Swindon.

"Luke's collecting Blessing from the Ferris's farm, guv," said Neil. "We should arrive at our designated points together, give or take. Alex and Lydia only have to drive over from Chippenham."

"Jake's meeting us at the rendezvous point, is he?" asked Gus.

"He contacted the landlord at the pub to tell him we'd be using his car park for an hour or two. Once Jake told him we were driving unmarked cars, he was fine."

"Is Jake bringing reinforcements?"

"Jake will have people covering the potential exits once

our targets are inside the perimeter, guv," said Neil. "He knows what to do."

"I hope I've got this right, Neil," said Gus. "Or I'm going to look a right idiot."

Neil turned off the main road into the pub car park and saw the flick of a headlight ahead.

"Jake's here, guv. Sunset is at nine o'clock. It won't be long now."

"One way or the other," growled Gus as they got out of the car.

"Nervous, Gus?" asked Jake Latimer. "I know you've done this a hundred times before, but not for a while."

"Are you alone?" asked Gus.

"No, I brought a friend," said Jake.

As Gus got nearer to Jake's car, he recognised PCSO Travers.

"Is he any good in a fight?" asked Gus.

"Taekwondo," said Jake. "Only a red belt so far, but he's keen."

"Did Gareth Francis agree to help out?" asked Gus.

"He would have liked to be here, but he's taken a DS. So he's awaiting your call."

"Let's get into position then, gents," said Neil. "A quick comms check. Are you receiving me?"

Alex and Luke replied in the affirmative.

A brisk walk through Rushey Platt Park brought the four men to the nature reserve.

Darkness enveloped them as they spread out as far from the canal bank as possible. Their dark clothing and face masks meant that anyone on the footpath would be unaware of their presence.

"Target A is en route," said Alex.

"Target A will approach your sector in fifteen minutes," said Jake. "Traffic control teams, on standby."

"Target B has left the house," said Luke.

"Stand by for further orders," said Gus.

The park was empty and eerily quiet. Gus expected birds to be fluttering and animals scurrying along the canal bank. Even a courting couple that Jake would need to send packing, but there was nothing.

Gus sensed the first twinge of cramp in his right calf. He wasn't used to crouching for long periods. Gus eased his leg out from under him and massaged the affected area. In the distance, he heard a car door shut.

A dark, hooded figure appeared from the entrance to the nature reserve and strolled along the footpath. Target A looked over their shoulder every twenty yards.

Gus switched his attention to the left, where a bright light pierced the darkness.

Target B was on their way.

The two figures stopped by the canal bank and spoke a few words. Gus couldn't hear what they said, but a package passed between them. In seconds, the two figures had turned to leave.

"Go! Go! Go!" shouted Neil.

Jake Latimer and Travers had reached the hooded figure and cuffed him before he could escape or discard the package he held.

Neil had sprinted to the footpath to intercept the cyclist.

He shone his torch into her face.

"Stop where you are, Debbie. The game's up."

Debbie let her bicycle drop to the floor. She was in shock.

"Blessing, can you hear me?" said Gus.

"Yes, guv,"

"Check Lucy is alright. She can't stay in the house alone. Get Luke to contact Mary Bennett and drop Lucy off in Penhill. She'll take care of her tonight."

"Got it, guv," said Blessing.

"It worked like clockwork, guv," said Neil.

"You didn't have cause to be nervous, Gus," said Jake. "It was just as you thought."

"What was in the package, Travers?" asked Neil, staring at the man in handcuffs.

"Until we get the contents checked for concealments, they purport to be machine parts from Brazil," said Travers. "The packaging indicates the items were destined for RJNM Engineering, guv."

"I suspect we'll discover equipment in one of those outbuildings which Maidment used to retrieve the heroin," said Gus. "Any other signs of engineering work will just be camouflage for what's really going on."

"Our drug dealer didn't want his product delivered to his door," said Gus, "Debbie working at Dorcan meant they could arrange a system whereby she intercepted packages and carried them home on her bicycle panniers."

"On a Friday," said Neil. "The extra weight slowed Debbie's return journey."

"I'm confused," said Jake. "I thought you reckoned James Neville, the father of Ryan Lock, was the dealer. So where did this chap enter the equation?"

"Take a closer look," said Gus. "Say hello to Rodney James Neville Maidment. Shall I take you through the events as I see things?"

"I think you had better," said Jake. He called for two cars to leave the blockade and come to collect the prisoners.

Jake, Travers, Neil, and Gus were back in the pub car park several minutes later.

"One more thing before I start," said Gus getting his phone from his pocket. "Gareth? Go ahead and take the statement. They have nothing to fear now."

"Come on, guv," said Neil, "time to explain."

"Maidment arrived in Swindon in 2000 and targeted the young Karen Lock," said Gus. "He'd hardly tell her his proper name, would he, when the object of the exercise was rape. Maidment left in 2001 after learning Karen was pregnant. Maidment couldn't have moved far away because he started work at Honda. During his second spell hunting for victims in town, he met the promiscuous Debbie Read. We never got Debbie to admit whether she took several lovers between 2002 and 2007 when Pat walked out. A paternity test will prove the point. Lucy is Maidment's child. I looked at Ryan Lock as a babe-in-arms in the photo his mother supplied and compared it to Lucy's photo from Mary Bennett's collection. The eyes have it, as they say."

"Debbie admitted she'd lied to us, guv," said Neil. "But she didn't move the dates she spent with Maidment back to a time before Pat walked out."

"No, she admitted they had met up again just before Christmas 2012, and things continued for ten months. Debbie's words to Luke were that they had seen one another for a while *before*. When he asked when that was, Debbie said it was eighteen months after Pat left. That may have been true, but one look at those photographs, and you can see that she omitted to tell Luke this personal relationship has been going on for years."

"When did the drug dealing enter the equation?" asked Jake.

"I suspect it was after December 2012," said Gus. "Ryan Lock will give us details of the first time his father met him outside school. According to his history, Maidment targeted schoolchildren in the town for more than one purpose. Stacey Read spotted an older man with her best friend, Ryan, and investigated. Stacey was an intelligent girl; it wasn't long before she realised they were father and son. Remember what Vanessa Nicholls and Mary Bennett told us. Stacey asked if it was her fault her father had walked out. Vanessa and Mary told her not to blame herself. What was Stacey's response? I knew it. Dad left because of Lucy. Unfortunately, neither woman picked up on the true meaning of that."

"They thought they'd dealt with her concerns," said Neil.

"When Maidment and Debbie split up in October 2013. He went straight to Vanessa," said Gus. "Debbie hasn't told us whether any of her lovers saw Stacey at the house in Gorse Hill, but Vanessa admitted Maidment might have bumped into her when they were together. Stacey recognised him as the man pestering Ryan and selling him drugs. She already suspected Lucy was that man's daughter and worried he would try to manipulate Lucy too. The lone visits to Vanessa's house were to protect Lucy. True to form, Maidment took one look at Stacey Read, and she became a target, just as Karen Lock had fourteen years earlier."

"How did things play out here in the nature reserve then, Gus?" asked Jake.

"I could never fathom why Stacey didn't run back towards the entrance," said Gus. "When I worked it out, it made this case far worse than I ever imagined. Ryan will fill in the sequence of events when he gives his statement to Gareth Francis. I won't hypothesise. I'll wait until the facts appear on my desk in the morning."

Epilogue

GARETH FRANCIS CALLED Gus first thing. An email arrived in his inbox one minute later, which contained a copy of Ryan Lock's statement.

> *I waited with Stacey in the cold and dark until my father arrived. I stayed hidden when Stacey ran from our hiding place and shone the torch in my Dad's face. Then she took the photo. My Dad recognised Stacey and realised I told her he would be there that night.*
>
> *He shouted my name and told me I was a goner. I didn't move; I couldn't let him know I was there, watching. Dad laughed and told Stacey he would do what I should have done by now. Stacey stood frozen on the spot holding the torch and the phone. He grabbed her coat, undid it, and I heard Stacey scream as he touched her.*
>
> *I saw the torch spinning out of her hand into the grass. In the torch beam, I saw Dad holding her coat in one hand. I heard Stacey running away, but she stumbled and fell. Dad must have found the knife in her coat pocket. He ran after Stacey, and I heard her cry*

214

when he stabbed her. Dad was still trying to get her clothes off, but somehow Stacey got free and made it onto the footpath. I could hear her footsteps.

I wanted to yell at her to come towards me, hoping we could fight him off together, but Stacey saw a bright light in front of her a hundred yards away. It was a cyclist. It must have been the person my Dad was meeting. Unfortunately, I couldn't tell who it was; they wore a hooded jacket and a helmet.

Stacey screamed once more. It was a dreadful sound. The cyclist turned off the headlamp, and it was pitch black. The police reckoned Stacey fell into the canal because the stab wounds weakened her. It wasn't easy to make out, but they pushed her in and stood watching until everything went quiet.

Next, my Dad and the other person seemed to be looking for something. They retraced my Dad's steps and must have collected the phone, the torch, and Stacey's bag. I waited until they had gone before creeping home to Mum. When I told her what I'd seen, she told me to remember what my Dad had said. I was a goner if he knew I'd been there. I did my best to get caught soon after that. It was safer here than on the streets in Swindon.

Gus heard the lift descend to the ground floor. The team would soon share the news. Stacey's agonised scream came when she realised the cyclist was not her saviour.

"Did Gareth provide the telling blow?" said Neil as the others gathered around.

"He did, Neil," said Gus. "I learned a salutary lesson from this case."

"What, guv?" said Neil.

"All things bright aren't always beautiful."

A perfect couple's dark secrets. A murder that shatters everything.

The murder of Alan Duncan during his weekly run sets Gus Freeman and the Crime Review Team on a path to unravel a complex web of deceit. As they delve into Alan's relationship with Maddy Mills, they discover that the couple's seemingly perfect life may have been built on a foundation of lies.

Turn the page for a free preview…

Buried Secrets: Chapter One

Wednesday, 21 May 2008

Alan Duncan left his home in Cuttle Lane, Biddestone, at six-thirty in the evening. His partner, Madeleine Mills, known to those who knew her as Maddy, watched him walk to the gateway. She turned away as Alan eased into a steady jog and set off on his regular midweek run. She had their two-bedroomed semi-detached home to herself for ninety minutes.

The couple had met in Chippenham four years ago at a leaving party for one of her call centre colleagues, Anna Phillips. For eleven years, Anna and Maddy had shared a desk. That party had been the last place Maddy wanted to be, but Alan had arrived with Wayne, Anna's husband.

Maddy suspected Anna and her husband had planned this so-called chance encounter for several weeks. As the evening progressed, however, she relaxed and enjoyed Alan's company. In his own words, he joined the Royal Navy at eighteen to see the world. But, unfortunately, the magic had worn off after a dozen years. So on his thirtieth birthday, he moved from the high seas to work for a Corsham firm as a draughtsman.

"What on earth attracted you to Corsham?" she had asked him.

"I was born there. My parents still live in the town, and my father, Bob, spotted an advert on the work's canteen noticeboard. It was pure luck. I had many skills they were looking for, and the family connection didn't hurt. Dad has worked there for over thirty years. Finally, his firm agreed to give me a shot. Wayne suggested I come with him tonight to celebrate. I heard this afternoon that my three-month trial was successful. I'm official as from Monday morning."

When Alan kissed her goodnight at the end of the evening, he'd asked to see her again. They hadn't spent more than a day apart in the past four years.

After Maddy finished her chores, she caught up on one of her favourite TV shows. She reminisced that any thoughts of avoiding a new relationship had disappeared within weeks of that leaving party. The couple had moved here to Biddestone together after four months. Village life, a handful of miles from their workplaces, suited them down to the ground.

Maddy's friend, Anna, had had three enjoyable years with her new job in Swindon, but Joshua's arrival last December had put a temporary hold on her career. Maddy and Alan had agreed to be the boy's godparents if Wayne and Anna ever got around to arranging a christening. Maddy had already driven to the Phillips's home in Cepen Park, Chippenham, to babysit frequently. For Maddy and Alan, there was still time, but they were enjoying life as a couple. There was no pressure.

Maddy had worked at the same company on the

Bumpers Farm Industrial Estate on the outskirts of Chippenham for fifteen years. Alan was plodding along at his job in Corsham. It might have seemed an ordinary existence to many, but Maddy had learned from experience that wild fluctuations of highs and lows were overrated.

Alan had kept fit during his time in the Navy. As he told Maddy, he had little choice, and in the past four years, her partner had maintained a regular exercise regime. Alan loved to run around the village lanes but had never attempted to persuade Maddy to join him. She told him the housework she did while he ran kept her figure trim.

Wayne and Alan were still firm friends and shared a common interest. But, in Anna and Maddy's opinion, it was more of a passion. Their men were keen cyclists with high-spec bikes, helmets, and the ubiquitous lycra clothing that accompanied it. So on weekends, Wayne drove across from Cepen Park with his bicycle on a frame attached to their car's boot. Then he and Alan disappeared for three hours.

Maddy and Anna reckoned that the distances they covered were like the fisherman's tale about the size of the one that got away. There was no escaping the facts; they were both fit individuals for men in their mid-thirties.

Maddy finished watching her programme and checked her watch. Almost eight o'clock. Alan would soon be home. Before joining her in the lounge, he would shower and don a fresh t-shirt and shorts. It was rare for Alan to wear long trousers at home, except in the dead of winter. He told Maddy that wearing a suit during the working week was bad enough. He'd had his fill of uniforms.

Alan Duncan jogged along Church Road and turned the corner towards home. He usually enjoyed his weekly run, but tonight something had unsettled him. As Alan reached the Crown Inn at Giddeahall on the outward leg, a man sat in the beer garden pointed at him. Then he tapped his nose. As Alan turned back into the village, he was sure he heard the man say, "You can run, but you can't hide."

The man was a stranger. Alan didn't look back to confirm that he'd heard the comment. Instead, he dismissed it as the ramblings of someone who had been sitting in the beer garden since lunchtime, and was drunk.

Alan closed the garden gate behind him as a Vauxhall Zafira cruised past. He watched as the car disappeared along the lane. Alan couldn't recall their neighbours driving a Zafira, but why did the driver look familiar?

As he ran upstairs to the bathroom, he tripped on the last step, ending up on all-fours on the landing.

Maddy appeared in the lounge doorway.

"Are you okay, Alan?" she called.

"Yeah, don't worry, sweetheart. I forgot there were fourteen stairs. Give me ten minutes. I'll be with you."

Maddy returned to her seat, and Alan took his shower. As the water cascaded over him, he realised why the driver seemed familiar.

Saturday, 24 May 2008

"What time is Wayne picking you up today?" asked Maddy.

"He wants to be on the road by one o'clock," said Alan. "I ate a good meal last night and plan a high-carb breakfast to get me through today's session. What will you be doing?"

"Can you come with me to do the weekly shopping this morning?" asked Maddy.

"No problem. We won't need anything for tomorrow, don't forget. We promised to go to my Mum and Dad for dinner. I can rely on Mum feeding us until we're fit to burst. I don't think she believes we can cater for ourselves."

"I remember. As for later, Anna might appreciate a visit," said Maddy.

"No doubt you'll offer to give Joshua a cuddle to ease her burden."

Maddy had pulled a face, thrown Alan the car keys, and he'd driven them to the Morrison's supermarket on the A350.

"Is this the route you took on Wednesday evening?" asked Maddy.

"Mmm," replied Alan. "I doubled back at the Crown. This supermarket is brilliant for us, isn't it? Only a ten-minute drive from home, and we never get snarled up in those interminable traffic jams through the centre of Chippenham."

"Hark at you," laughed Maddy. "I've got the devil of a job to get you to come shopping with me most weekends. Or did you want to change the subject? What happened, Alan? Did you decide to stop at the Crown for a crafty pint on a warm evening?"

"No, nothing like that," he replied as he searched the car park for an empty space.

An hour later, they drove home. Alan kept checking his mirror but saw nothing.

Wayne sounded his horn as he drove past the house at a quarter to one, turned his car around in a gateway and idled back. Alan was in the lane with his bike, waiting. He stood and watched his friend detach his bike from the rack.

"A good day for it," said Wayne. "Are you sure you're ready?"

"Warmley via the Cotswold Way and then back on the A420," said Alan. "You bet I'm ready. It should take us two-and-a-half hours. I can't think of a better way to spend a Saturday afternoon."

"It's a route we haven't tried before," said Wayne. "We must be ultra-careful on the busy main road. Don't worry; I'll look after you."

"Yeah, right," laughed Alan. "Let's get going."

Alan checked the Crown's car park and beer garden as they cycled past. There was no sign of the Zafira or its driver.

After two-and-a-half hours of steady cycling, Wayne followed Alan back into Biddestone. They were both tired but satisfied with their afternoon's work. Wayne noticed a man by The Green standing by his car, waving. Ahead of him, Alan cycled harder. Wayne puffed out his cheeks.

"Give me a break, Alan," he called, "I'm shattered. Who was that guy, anyway? Did you know him?"

"I saw no one," Alan replied.

That was odd, thought Wayne. He looked straight at us.

Maddy had just arrived home when they pulled up outside the house. She watched as Wayne re-racked his bike.

"How was Joshua?" he asked.

"He slept most of the time I was there," said Maddy.

"Never mind, sweetheart," said Alan.

"Typical," said Wayne. "He'll be awake half the night now."

"You love it, really," said Maddy.

Wayne grinned, and with a cheery wave, he drove home.

"Someone's going to sleep well tonight," said Maddy as she watched Alan wheel his bike up the garden path.

Alan wished that were true. As tired as he was. he couldn't stop wondering what the guy in the Zafira wanted. He'd imagined that Wednesday evening could have been a random event. How did the guy know to be in the village this afternoon as they returned from their cycle ride?

Sunday, 25 May 2008

Maddy drove them to Corsham for Sunday lunch with Alan's parents. Bob and Elizabeth were always pleased to see them. Alan was an only child. Maddy had a brother, Darren, and her parents lived in a village outside Leeds. Maddy had left home at eighteen and wasn't in a rush to return. She kept in touch with her family members with a few words in a Christmas card. Years ago, the family had decided they had their own lives to lead.

Alan and Maddy knew what to expect when they came to the Duncan family home. A Sunday roast with all the trimmings, plus a long list of questions about work, marriage, holidays, children, and did they want the second helping of rhubarb and custard now or after their tea?

When they left at seven o'clock, Alan was glad to escape.

"Sorry if they went on a bit, Maddy," he said.

"I don't mind," said Maddy, "they care about you. Your Dad will retire at sixty next year, from what he said. So it's only natural they want to see we're financially secure. Any spare cash they have will get spent on foreign holidays; they won't want to dig deep to get us out of a hole. As for any wedding, your Dad probably thinks that because of the distance I've put between myself and my family, they wouldn't be much help. He's right, but we're happy as we are, aren't we?"

"Happy as pigs in the proverbial," said Alan.

Grab your copy…
vinci-books.com/buriedsecrets

About the Author

Ted Tayler is the international bestselling indie author of The Freeman Files and The Phoenix series. Ted lives in the English west country, where his stories are based. He was born in 1945 and has been married to Lynne since 1971. They have three children and four grandchildren.

His thought-provoking mysteries appeal to readers of Sally Rigby, Joy Ellis, Pauline Rowson, and Faith Martin. His action-packed thrillers are a must for fans of Mark Dawson and J. C. Ryan.

Gus Freeman's cold case investigations are carried out with reasoned deduction rather than bursts of frantic action. In each of the twenty-four books, unsolved murder is accompanied by romance, humor, and country life. The core message in the twelve Phoenix novels is that criminals should pay for their crimes. Unfortunately, the current system fails to deliver the correct punishment, so Phoenix helps redress the balance.

Acknowledgments

The love and support of my family; without them, this would have been impossible.